HIGH TAR BABIES

FOR JOHN AND PETER

HIGH TAR BABIES
race hatred slavery love

by

MARCUS WOOD

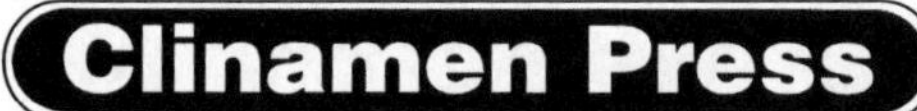

This publication is only possible due to a Grant in the Performing Arts from the Arts and Humainties Research Board and sponsorship from the Elephant Trust

Published 2001 by
Clinamen Press Limited
Enterprise House
Whitworth Street West
Manchester M1 5WG

www.clinamen.co.uk

A catalogue record for this book is available from the British Library

ISBN1 903083 83 4

1 3 5 7 9 8 6 4 2

Typeset in Clearface with Bauhaus and Meta display by
Northern Phototypesetting Co. Ltd., Bolton
Printed and bound in South Wales by
Creative Print and Design, Ebbw Vale

PICTURES

Picture 1   Cry Baby Tar Baby One   7
Picture 2   Cry Baby Tar Baby Two   8
Picture 3   Cry Baby Tar Baby Three   9
Picture 4   Assorted Tar Babies   10
Picture 5   Stork Tar Baby   12
Picture 6   Penguin Tar Baby One   13
Picture 7   Crow Tar Baby   14
Picture 8   Penguin Tar Baby Two   15
Picture 9   Vulture Tar Baby   16
Picture 10   Slug Tar Babies   17
Picture 11   Snail Tar Baby One   18
Picture 12   Snail Tar Baby Two   19
Picture 13   Wood Louse Tar Baby   20
Picture 14   Beetle Tar Baby One   21
Picture 15   Beetle Tar Baby Two   22
Picture 16   Beetle Tar Baby Three   23
Picture 17   Mayfly Tar Baby   24
Picture 18   Queen Termite Tar Baby   25
Picture 19   Soldier Termite Tar Baby   26
Picture 20   Stick Insect Tar Baby One   27
Picture 21   Stick Insect Tar Baby Two   28
Picture 22   Moth Tar Baby   29
Picture 23   Butterfly Tar Baby   30
Picture 24   Porcupine Tar Baby   31
Picture 25   Manatee Tar Baby One   32
Picture 26   Manatee Tar Baby Two   33
Picture 27   Giraffe Tar Baby   34
Picture 28   Hippopotamus Tar Baby   35
Picture 29   Elephant Tar Baby   36
Picture 30   Tar Telephone Strangled by its Own Cord One   37
Picture 31   Tar Telephone Strangled by its Own Cord Two   38
Picture 32   Tar Telephone Strangled by its Own Cord Three   39
Picture 33   Telephone Tar Baby   40

Picture 34   Slave Mask Tar Baby One   41
Picture 35   Slave Mask Tar Baby Two   42
Picture 36   Slave Mask Tar Baby Three   43
Picture 37   Tar Pit Tar Baby   44
Picture 38   Tar Baby Tar Baby   45

THIRTEEN WAYS OF LOOKING AT HIGH TAR BABIES
race hatred slavery and love

Brer Fox went ter wuk en got 'im some tar, en mix it wid some turkentime, en fix up a contrapshun what he call a Tar-Baby, en he took dish yer Tar-Baby en he sot 'er in de big road.

ON TAR

BY GEORGE BERKELEY

Hail vulgar juice of never-fading pine!
Cheap as thou art, thy virtues are divine.
To shew them and explain (such is thy store)
There needs much modern and much ancient lore.
While with slow pains we search the healing spell,
Those sparks of life that in thy balsam dwell,
From lowest earth by gentle steps we rise
Through air, fire, æther to the highest skies.
Things gross and low present truth's sacred clue
Sense, fancy, reason, intellect pursue
Her winding mazes, and by Nature's laws
From plain effects trace out the mystic cause,
And principles explore, though wrapt in shades,
That spring of life which the great world pervades,
The spirit that moves, the Intellect that guides,
Th'eternal One that o'er the Whole presides.
Go learn'd mechanic, stare with stupid eyes,
Attribute to all figure, weight and size;
Nor look behind the moving scene to see
What gives each wondrous form its energy.
Vain images possess the sensual mind,
To real agents and true causes blind.
But soon as intellect's bright sun displays
O'er the benighted orb his fulgent rays,
Delusive phantoms fly before the light,
Nature and truth lie open at the sight
Causes connect with effects supply
A golden chain whose radiant links on high
Fix'd to the sovereign throne from thence descend
And reach e'en down to tar the nether end.

Why Tar? What is the cultural currency of tar now? Tar, the body of this argument, has been in and around the human for a long time. Tar is versatile, a difficult thing to tie down. It has many histories and involves many stories. Here are some of them.

One. Tar is Smoking. There is an image problem, which the peace pipe has failed to cure. Pipes, cigars and beyond the horizon cigarettes, billions and billions of them, all smoking. Smoking tar has killed more people than war. Why do people still smoke, now they know that at best it will 'seriously damage your health'? Cigarette packets are like guns, objects which advertise their capacity to kill people efficiently. Why this celebration of death, linked to those funny height adjectives high, low, middle; was it the fault of Walter Raleigh? Potatoes and tobacco, Golden Wonder, is it a match for a cigar called Hamlet? Why did Raleigh end up on a bicycle and Hamlet on a cigar.

Two. Tar is terror. A language of fear, headlines to frighten on billboards, in colour supplements, on cigarette packets. Translate them how you like, the words 'low' 'middle' or 'high' turn aspiration on its head, give new depths to inspiration reinvented as emphysema and lung cancer. Images of horror children carry out of school, and around with them for the rest of their days – one the holocaust, two hard drugs, three venereal disease, four the disease of smoking. The healthy lung and the smoker's lung, one pink and perky, the other like a gigantic dried out banana skin dipped in molasses. A horrible thing, a hot thing, a living death. And when the smoker's lung lies down to rest, all the tar slowly levels out, an obscene tidal flow. What a thing it is, the smoker's lung.

Three. Tar is Driving. Tar means big business: engineering and building works, roofing and road surfacing. It marks the boundary of the civilised world, 'Both roads were dirt, the tar ended miles back' it says in the dictionary. Roads, motorways, three lane, four, five, six, seven, eight, how big can they get? Spaghetti junction, and all that spaghetti made of tar, dry and black, like that squid ink pasta. Roundabouts, playgrounds, parking lots and pavements, paths, and more roads, millions and millions of miles of them. Tar, tar, the stuff that cars run over, the stuff roads are made out of, the stuff that ruined the planet, and stitched us all up in a network of black lines, ebony veins of progress from the jungles of Brazil to the junctions of Brighton. But so beautiful, at first, new born, steam rollers pressing down soft spongy fragrant gravel onto a base of shining black paint as slick as cream, thick black cream. Then again, that sudden meaty and acrid aroma steaming out of a fenced off area, a hole in the ground and a bubbling vat of pitch, sensual, brazen, you want to lick it, a giant soup tureen, an everyday witch's cauldron with dusty workmen, our new weird sisters, bending around it, boys from the black stuff.

Four. Tar is Sailing. Ships were stuck together with it, sealed with it, caulked with it, Columbus had some of the first ships to be stuck together with bitumen, without tar the New World would never have been discovered, or not by him anyway. Sailors dipped their hair in it, and became quite simply tars. And tar still means sailor, even in Hollywood films, Jack Tar as folkloric as Jack Frost, Jack Tar with iridescent black pig tail, a thing alive, or a screaming face turned to camera as the burned out stub of his leg is forced into the tar bucket, the decks painted red to hide the running blood. Catch it falling. How can that be, tar as disinfectant, tar as the enemy of all known germs, tar the black seal over a wound? Show your wound.

Five. Tar is Slick. Tar is inside and outside the boat. Crude oil, the very essence of tar, floating in huge baths across the sea. Black tankers of tar, vast black tombs, hulls gutted on the rocks, spilling their black guts, and now it floats from coast to coast, black coagulated lumps. Whole bays, and rocky shores, wrapped up in the stuff, shoals of fish drowned in it, colonies of birds tarred and feathered spontaneously in the their millions. Bathers sitting on beaches, rubbing and picking at the black smears on their legs, trying to pull lumps off their towels and their knickers. Nature's Tar Babies looking out to sea. What a business, burn it, spray it with soap from helicopters, set fire to it, bomb it, go to war with it, it does no good, still swaying, still hanging in the sea. A dark disaster and we have turned the oceans into our own liquid Tar Babies.

Six. Tar is a Baby. Tar is centrally absorbed into Western race discourse via the Tar Baby story. The Tar baby may look like anything. Whether it is a penguin, or a slug, a telephone strangled by its own cord, or a modern mummy made with bandages and wearing a mask, all Tar Babies come from the same stock, and share the same parents.

When Joel Chandler Harris set about his reknowned retelling of an ancient African oral tale, which had then been adapted on the slave plantations, he created a story which lies at the heart of how whites and blacks look at the power relations of slavery. He called it The Wonderful Tar Baby Story, and it is the first and most enigmatic of the tales of Uncle Remus. It really is wonderful if you think how it still stands at the fulcrum of race and hatred.

In Harris's original the Tar Baby is a 'contrapshun' made out of tar and turpentine by Brer Fox and set up in the middle of the road. This thing is immediately unspeakably offensive to Brer Rabbit. The basis of Brer Rabbit's ferocious response to the Tar Baby lies in the passivity of the object, the threat of stillness, quietness. Black, still and voiceless, the Tar Baby is an enigma. Brer Rabbit cannot tolerate a presence that will not respond to him, that gives nothing back, and gives nothing away, a presence defined by absence. Brer Rabbit's response is to get literally stuck into this black other, his nemesis. It is impossible to say what the Tar Baby stands for, if it stands for anything. It is a black space we must fill, or go around.

Brer Rabbit is the figure within plantation mythologies who represents black empowerment. Through wit and cunning he invariably triumphs over the larger powerful carnivores (the slave power) which constantly threaten his very life. So why should the figure who finally brings the heroic trickster low, be silent, female and completely black? Why should the intelligent rabbit, the cleverest rabbit of all time, much much smarter than Bugs Bunny, a figure constitutionally so instinctive in avoiding physical confrontations with his enemies, why should he desire to destroy this object? The question becomes even harder when we remember that the tar baby is a girl baby. Maybe that's the point, maybe he has to make her respond because she's a girl: 'De tar baby she ain't sayin' nuthin'... says Brer Rabbit sezee, 'ef you don't take off dat hat an tell me howdy, I'm gwineter bus' you wide open.' No way to treat a lady.

Seven. Tar is Hate. The Tar Baby has been hi-jacked in a white gnashing of teeth, and a terror of black and white sex. The Tar Baby becomes a he, a potent black virility trapping and transforming the passive white girl into a female Brer Rabbit energised by a rogue chromosome: 'She was one of those white women who cannot leave black men alone... Some questing chromosome within holds her sexually fast to the tar baby,' as somebody says in the Oxford English Dictionary.

Eight. **Tar is Love.** The tar baby has been taken away from such a scene and wonderfully remade and is now the power and beauty of black women. Toni Morrison's Tar Babies change all sex and meaning. One of them is power and beauty, an arrangement in black and yellow:

> The skin like tar against the canary yellow dress... the woman turned her head sharply around to the left and looked right at Jadine. Turned those eyes too beautiful for eyelashes on Jadine and with a small parting of her lips, shot an arrow of saliva between her teeth down to the pavement and the hearts below. Actually it didn't matter. When you have fallen in love, rage is superfluous; insult impossible. You mumble "bitch", but the hunger never moves, never closes. It is placed, open and always ready for another canary yellow dress, other tar-black fingers holding three white eggs.

Morrison creates other seductive Tar Babies, swamp women, Tar Sirens who call with an ancient life force to the thin, off-black, not white, and compromised Jadine, trying to make her see why tar is more beautiful than Picasso (why didn't Picasso paint Guernica in tar?). They call her into the swamp, the black bog, where the natural tar that is the soup of life bubbles away. Bog action duende, a dark place where life and death fuse: 'No point in looking down at the slime, it would make her think of worms or snakes or crocodiles'. When she escapes from the swamp the tar clings on for dear life.

No one is quite sure exactly what has go onto her, what this new Brer Rabbit has got stuck into, but it's clear enough, as clear as mud:

> "what the hell happened to you?" He ran to her and put the bottle on the seat. She didn't look up, just wiped her eyes and said, "I took a walk over there and fell in."
> "Fell in what? that looks like oil "I don't know, mud I guess, but it felt like jelly while I was in it. But it doesn't come off like jelly. It's drying and sticking". Son kneeled down and stroked her skin. The black stuff was shiny in places and where it was dry it was like mucilage.

Of course it was like mucilage, it is the stuff of life. And Jadine herself is a Tar Baby of sorts. She's got more than a touch of the tar brush about her. Don't count her out. Morrison tells us that tar is tricky stuff, it means one thing and another.

Nine. Tar is Immortality. Go back further and Tar becomes even stranger, our strange familiar. Maybe, just maybe, there is a little bit of tar in everyone, all of us Europeans. Fifteenth and sixteenth century doctors and alchemists knew that Mummies are encased in tar (the resinous gum in which many of the later mummies were coated turned black and shiny over the centuries). For two hundred years people were eating and drinking the magic tar, crazy Europe, a genuine cannibalistic mania. Positively guzzling powdered mummies, and the word mummy simply meant tar. Mummy, derived from the Persian word, **Mumia**, which meant tar. Fat and thin it was all around us and twice as thick. Sir John Falstaff, desperate for those Merry Wives of Windsor, stuck in filthy linen and sweating at the bottom of a washing basket, then thrown into the mud of the river Thames, is terrified that he will dissolve magically into a mass of tar, a giant mummy 'and what a thing should I have been, being a mountain of mummy', what a thing indeed — a giant, lecherous Tar Baby.

The mummy lurks in lyrics, John Donne fishes one out and gives us more tar and sex. Love's Alchemy ends in tar, the clearest statement that you shouldn't love women for their minds, but just for their bodies, and what a body: 'Hope not for mind in women; at their best / Sweetness and wit, they are but mummy possessed', yes indeed surely the meaning in here breaks down into 'don't look for intelligence in women, only look at their bodies, and when you finally get into that body, you will find that it's like possessing a corpse, an old Egyptian corpse.' The most frightening Tar Baby yet, a dead mummy for a lover, who can handle that? Stick that in your pipe and smoke it Sigmund Freud, who incidentally got lip cancer from smoking tar. Donne done for, surely death has a right to be proud this time.

The market for eating powdered mummies grew bigger, so insatiable were our progenitors that they started up mass production of fake Egyptian mummies to fill the need, to stop the gap. Washed up and dried out, Egyptians of all shapes and sizes in the seventeenth and eighteenth centuries, wrapped in bandages stuck in the sand and painted with tar by the thousand, more Tar Babies for the Western maw. Mummies picked up and carried off, thrown overboard passengers liners when they began to stink, set up in bars in the Wild West. Tar entered the European popular consciousness, body and soul, as a mysterious black powder. Could we be saturated with the immortal powers of the Egyptian Pharaohs, tar mummies, Tar Babies? ... in your dreams.

Ten. Tar is Water. But it didn't stop there. Having sated our taste for Tar we then developed an incredible thirst for it. Tar maintained a place within the medical culture of the West, in the eighteenth-century there was a craze for drinking tar water. Ask the great Bishop Berkeley, visual theorist and tar drinker, he was mad for it. Countless learned tracts sang its praises and miraculous health giving properties, quack medical companies made vast profits, and the European body became ever more absorbed with the stuff. 'High Tar' certainly, and a health warning that if you didn't imbibe it you might die. Inspiration.

Eleven. Tar is Torture. Tar is darker, meaner, more painful. Tar and torture, a black and white history of ritualised humiliation, pain and punishment. The image of an IRA informer leaning exhausted, maybe dead. A drooping lily in a vase, strapped with belts to a lamp post, stripped to the waist, clumps of white feathers embedded in the black mess that has been poured over his mask like face and fragile pale body. The first divinely and legally sanctioned paintings on the body with tar and feathers may have happened on boats going out to the Crusades. Richard the Lionheart drew up a punishment code for Crusaders: 'Laws of Richard I (Coeur de Lion) concerning Crusaders who were to go by sea 1189 A.D. "A robber moreover, convicted of theft, shall be shorn like a hired fighter, and boiling tar shall be poured over his head, and feathers from a cushion shall be shaken out over his head – so that he may be publicly known; and at the first land where the ships put in he shall be cast on shore." And Tar and Feathers flowed on, used outside the law, the peoples' verdict on the other, British tax gatherers and customs men tarred and feathered in Boston, abolitionists in the Deep South, sympathisers with Anti-Apartheid in South Africa. Black, sticky, hot and organic, tar is a strange substance with which to burn and stain enemies, body art as punishment. Ritually paint a body with hot tar and cover it with white feathers, why, what do the feathers mean? Are they the white feathers traditionally handed out to cowards? Do they tell us in some indirect way of a fallen Icarus, ultimate achievement reduced to a plucked chicken? Is this a black devil, Lucifer gone out, the angel wings torn and scattered like wild doves?

Twelve. Tar is Art. Why paint in black tar. Tar smells delicious, it feels great, it produces a tremendous tonal range from crystalline jetty blacks to golden ochres, it handles wonderfully and can be used treacle thick or water thin. But beyond this there is tradition. European masters painted with it way before Goya. It was not just roofs, fences and human bodies which tar had been painted over. From the late seventeenth century the fashion for the disastrous and sadistic night spaces of Magnasco and Salvator Rosa had allowed tar painting to find one form of its proper dark. Within the Academies, bitumen, asphalt, natural tar pigments, came into their own. The black crackling shells which now evolve, grow across, corrupt vast areas of the canvases of Joshua Reynolds, Fuseli, Charles Pinkham Ryder, not only exasperate restorers but bear testimony to the sheer weight of tar that was being lovingly caressed over canvasses for the last three hundred years. And a lot of this tar was made of mummies. If you had been looking down the garden of a certain house in the early 1820s, then one evening (this is a true story) you would have seen a distinguished painter walk down the path carrying tubes of paint and accompanied by a clergyman. The two men dig a small grave, and they place the tubes of paint within and the service for the burial of the dead is read. As the soil falls on the tubes you can read the labels and it says 'Mummy Brown' on them. This painter did not like the idea that he was painting with the un-consecrated bodies of ancient Egyptians, so finally he had to give those pasted bodies from the desert their just desserts, a decent Christian burial. Just think about it, the bodies of Egyptian men and women, and girls and boys, and babies, hanging in dark resinous veils across the bituminous surfaces of Rembrandts and Rosas, gently suspended across Turner's early Scottish nightscapes, a beautiful still darkness, calm not terror, presence not absence. More Tar Babies, calm and terrible High-Art-High-Tar babies.

Thirteen. Tar is Duende. Back to Goya. The Spanish surrealist poet and playwright Frederico Garcia Lorca, murdered by Franco's supporters during the Spanish civil war, tried to define the indefinable, the spirit of the duende. Only he would dare to do it. For Lorca the duende is finally something that exists underground, in the blackness beneath the surface: 'each art' he concludes 'has a duende of a different kind and form, but they all join their roots at a point where the "dark sounds"… emerge, ultimate matter, uncontrollable and quivering common foundation of wood, of sound, of canvas, and of words. "Dark sounds" behind which we discover in tender intimacy volcanoes, ants, gentle breezes.' One way to approach blackness in art is to try and see what these dark sounds might be. Within painting Lorca sees them at the end of Goya's life, where the duende only entered his work with blackness, quite explicitly the blackness of tar:

> To help us seek the duende there is neither map nor discipline. All one knows is that it burns
> like powdered glass, that is exhausts, that it rejects all the sweet geometry one has
> learned, that it breaks with all styles, that it compels Goya, master of greys, silvers, and
> of those pinks in the best English paintings, to paint with his knees and with his fists, hor-
> rible bitumen blacks

The black paintings of Goya's old age, as he worked on in syphilitic near oblivion, in
the Quinta del Sordo, the house of the deaf man, painting images which are black in
form, black in fact and black in-sight, are presented as an act of violence, a sublime
street fight with the materials of art, Goya beats the canvas up. Titian, in his old age,
is reported to have painted with his finger tips, in order to remove the physical barrier
between the paint and his senses, Goya doesn't stroke, he is shown not only punching but, bizarrely, kneeing, the canvas, like a crazy Brer Rabbit, enmeshing himself in
the Tar Baby, getting stuck with a blind violence ever more deeply in to the utterly black
substance which will control and pacify him. For Lorca, Goya combines art and a blind
but ecstatic fury, and in this black act joins himself with the darkness of the duende.
These paintings liberate blackness from the interpretative limitation of the Western
aesthetic, black is beyond good and bad, beautiful and ugly, right and wrong, it is the
blackness of blackness.

So Tar is it, it has the duende. If you want to make art about race torture, hatred or
love, about colour symbolism, about the mysteries of black and white, about sex and
colour Tar is your Alpha and Omega. So my show is a showing of Tar Babies. They are
authentic, made just as Brer fox made his original: 'Brer Fox went ter wuk en got 'im
some tar en mix it wid some turkentime, en fix up a contrapshun what he call a tar
baby, en he took dish yer Tar-Baby en he sot 'er in de big road.' How do you make tar
thin enough to draw with like ink. Mix it with turpentine. That is one explanation of my
work: Brer Fox, trying to catch Brer Rabbit, by hanging out in the middle of the big road
called the gallery a series of contraptions made of tar and turpentine, hoping Brer Rabbit will come along. Look but don't touch as an earlier Brer Foxe warns in his very violent Book of Martyrs. 'He that toucheth tar cannot but be defiled thereby'. But is that
a warning or a challenge, don't we desire defilement, because at the end of he day
tar is a mystery we want to bury ourselves in, tar is black and warm, tar is black and
comforting, so why does it appear so frightening? For a long time it has been lurking
there, meaning comfort, warmth, and life. Dinosaurs in California saunter up to it, and
get stuck in, and so we find them today with their black fossilised bones in the tar pit.
Tar is after all the life force itself, sex. Michel Foucault in the **History of Sexuality** stum-
bled across a new world, looking at Paulo Segneric's 'Guidebook for Penitents' he
uncovers how tar has, at the end of the seventeenth century, come to constitute a terrifying metaphor for sexual activity. Sex in all its varieties, details, in all its unrecover-
ability, is tar. Tar is equated with the sexual obsession at the heart of the act of Catholic
confession, the 'unclean' thoughts which are the adhesive between confessor and con-
fessee are nothing less than tar:

> Little by little, the nakedness of the questions formulated by the confession manuals of the
> Middle Ages, and a good number of those still in use in the seventeenth century was veiled.
> One avoided entering into that degree of detail which some authors... had for a long time
> believed indispensable for the confession to be complete, description of the respective posi-
> tions of the partners, the postures assumed, gesture, places touched, caresses the precise
> moment of pleasure- an entire painstaking review of the sexual act in its very unfolding. Dis-
> cretion was advised, with increasing emphasis. The greatest reserve was counselled when
> dealing with sins against purity. 'This matter is similar to tar, for, however one might handle
> it, even to cast it far from oneself, it sticks nonetheless, and always soils

Maybe now it is time to positively advance that unclean contact, to get stuck into it, to
see a terrible beauty in the idea of painting black. Why not begin with: 'A golden chain
whose radiance links on high' and 'from thence descend/And reach e'en down to tar
the nether end.'

PICTURES

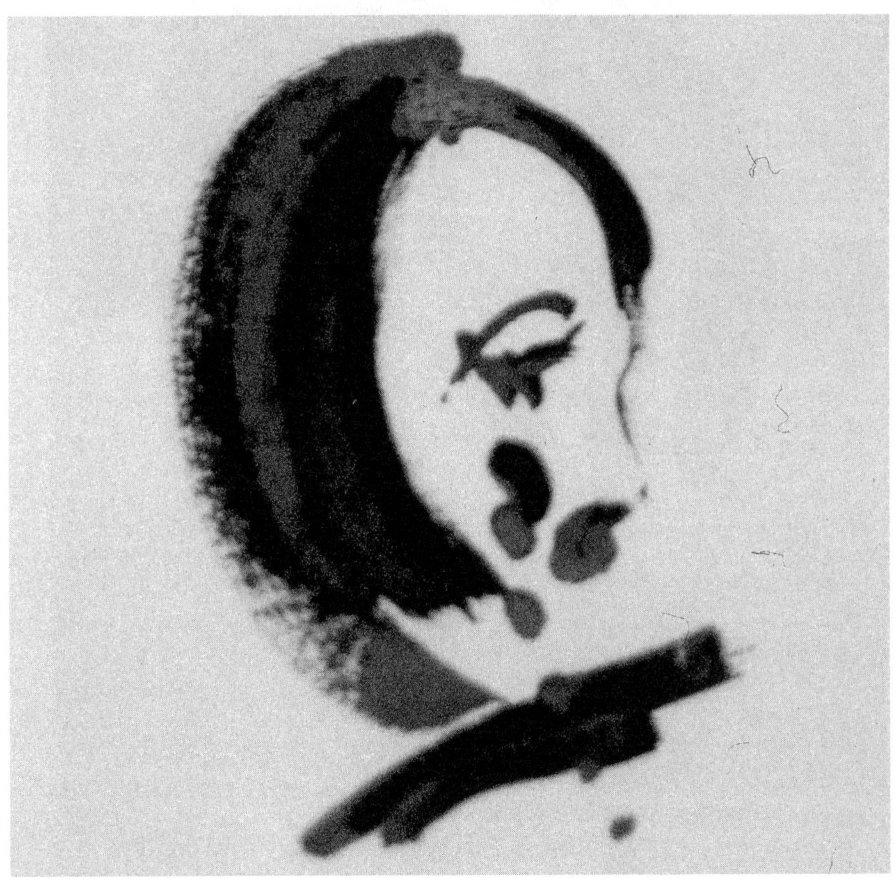

1 Cry Baby Tar Baby One

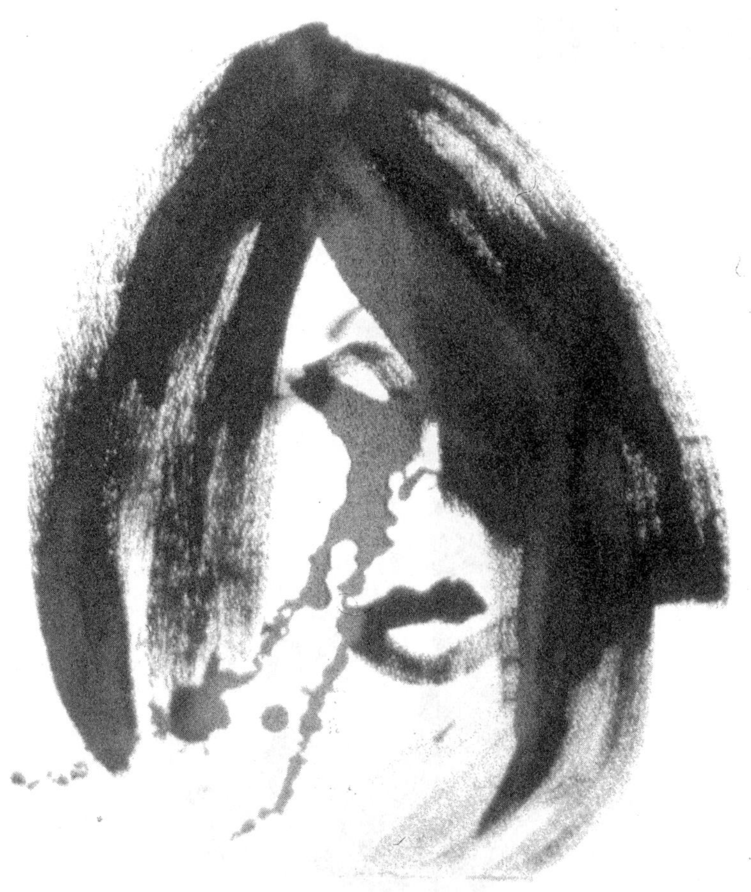

2 Cry Baby Tar Baby Two

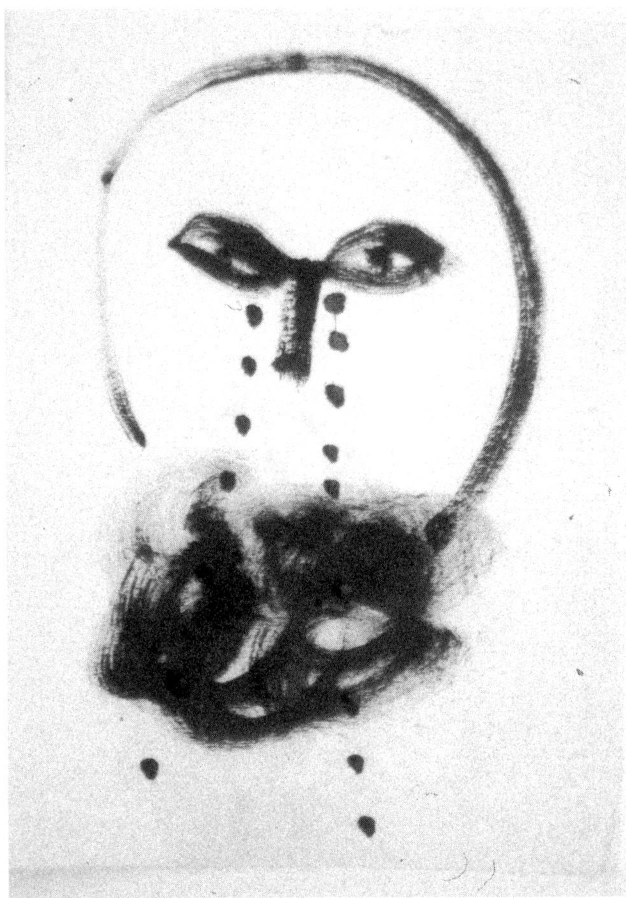

3 Cry Baby Tar Baby Three

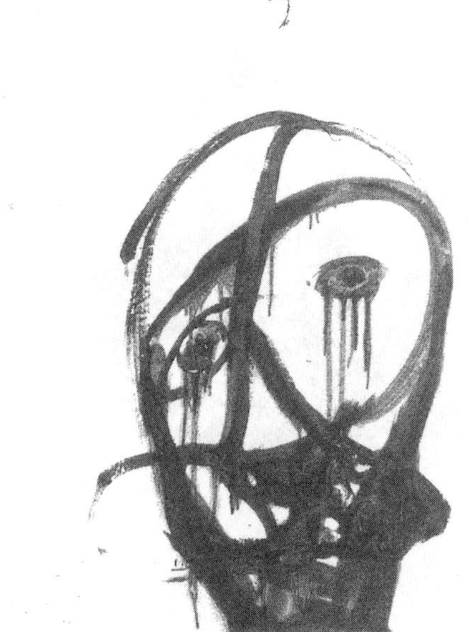

4 Assorted Tar Babies

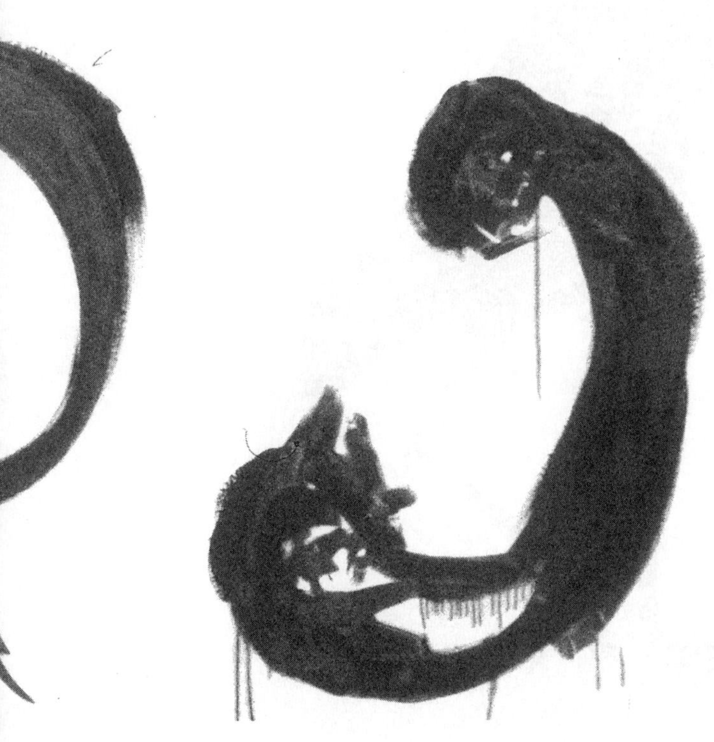

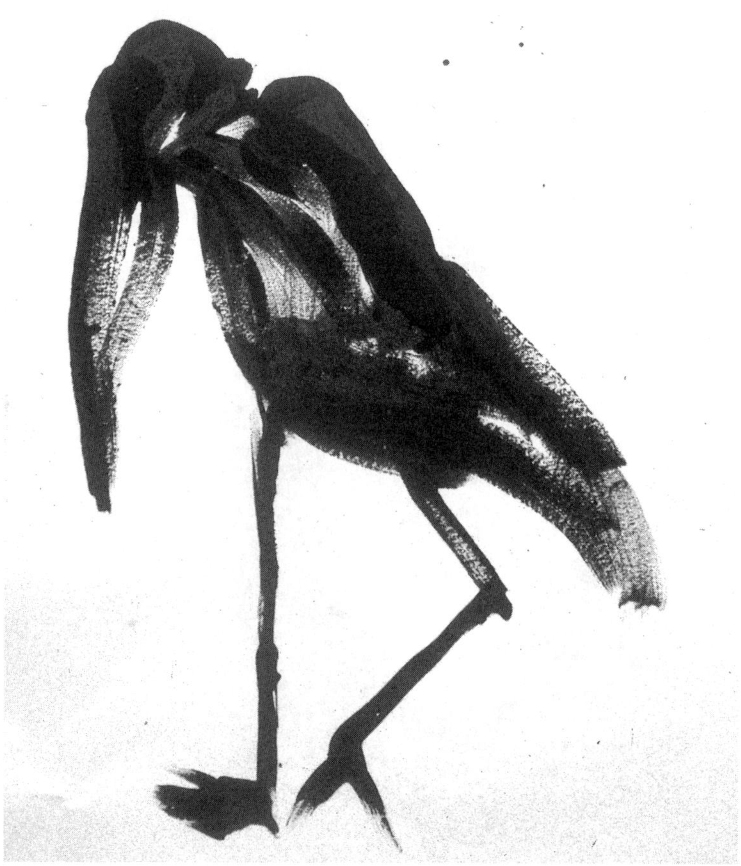

5 Stork Tar Baby

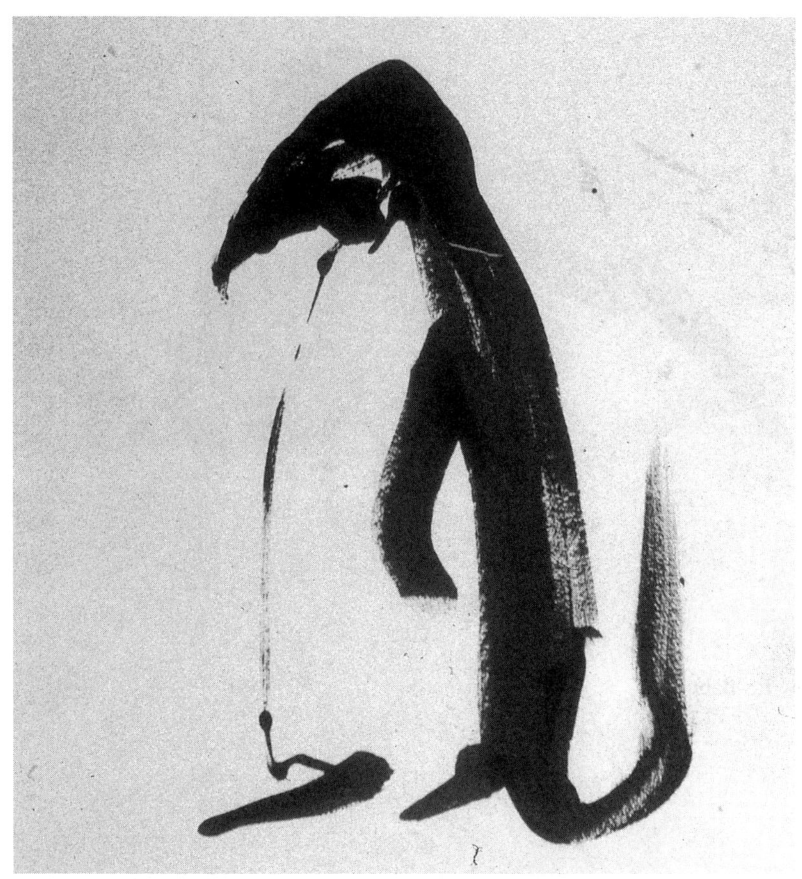

6 Penguin Tar Baby One

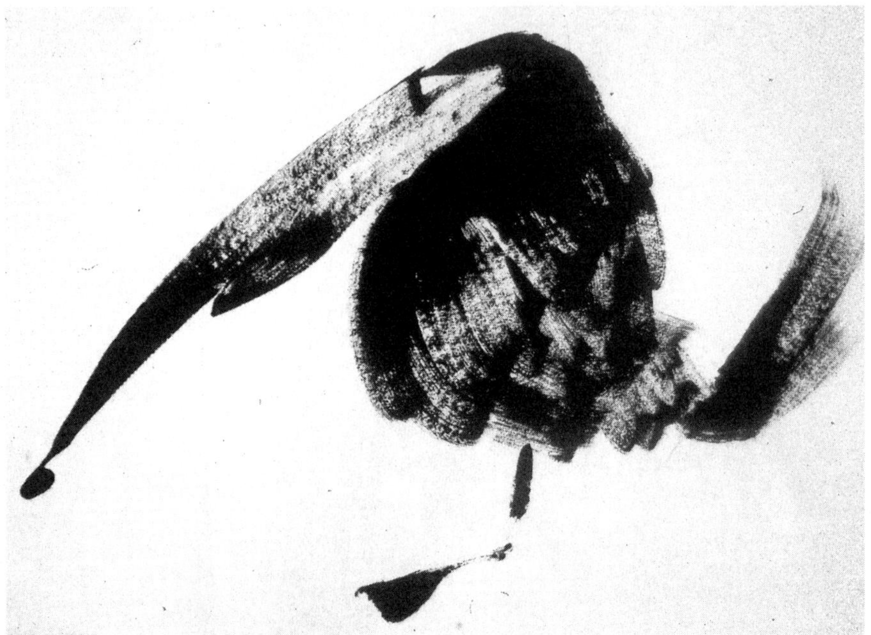

7 Crow Tar Baby

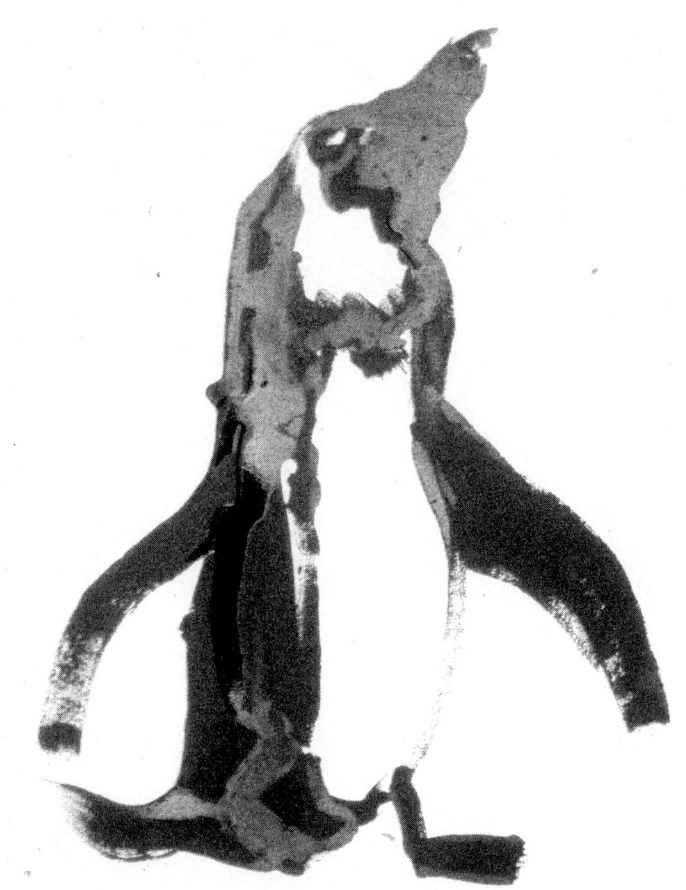

8 Penguin Tar Baby Two

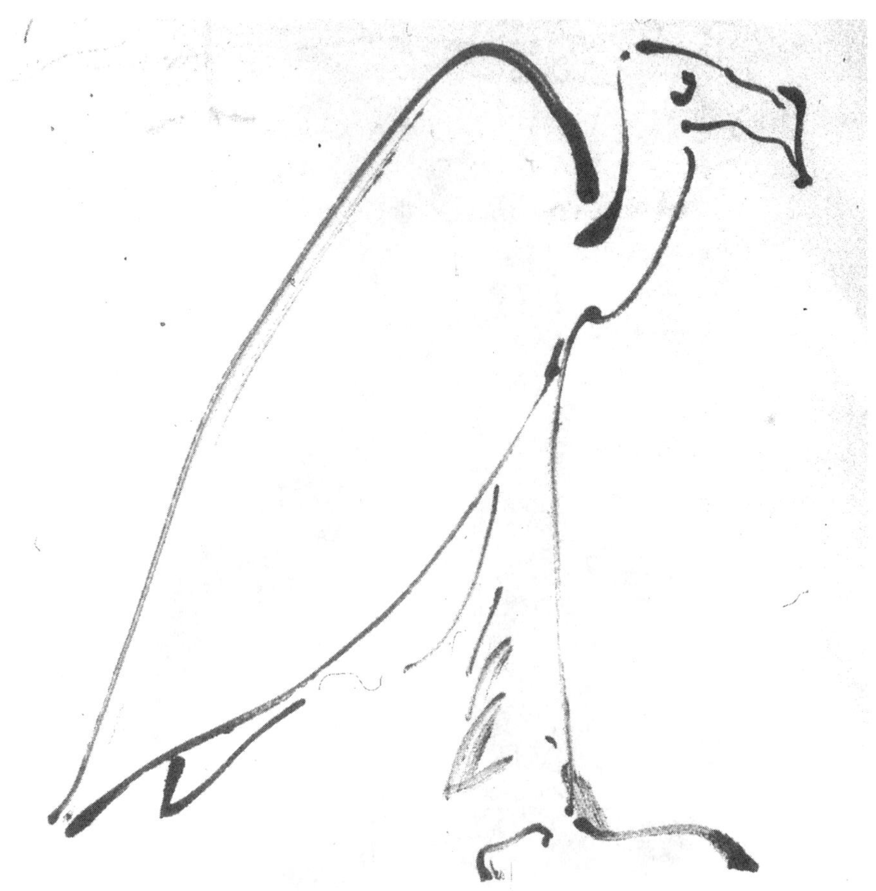

9 Tar Baby Vulture

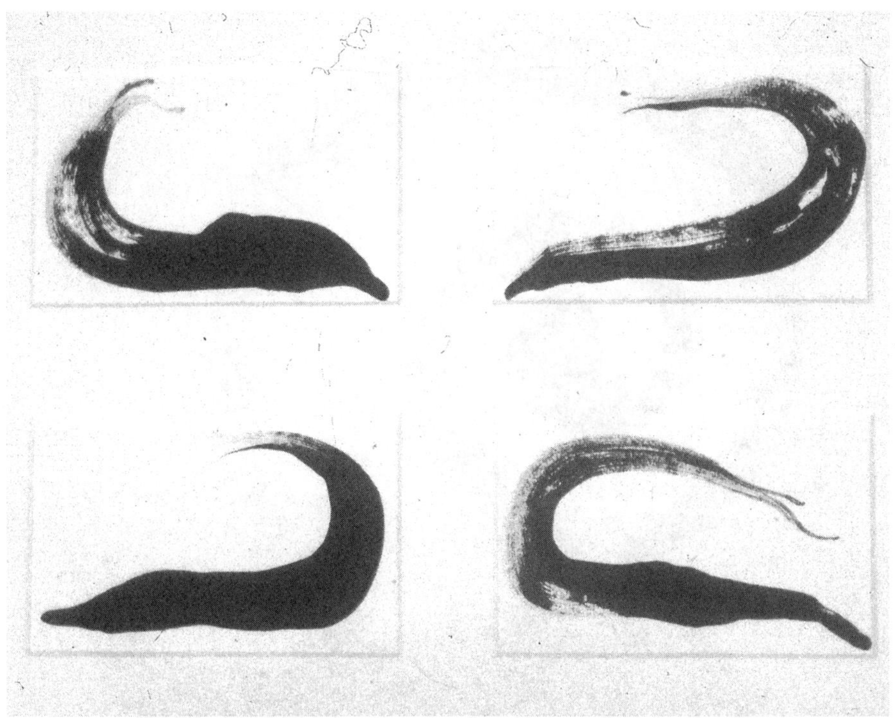

10 Slug Tar Babies

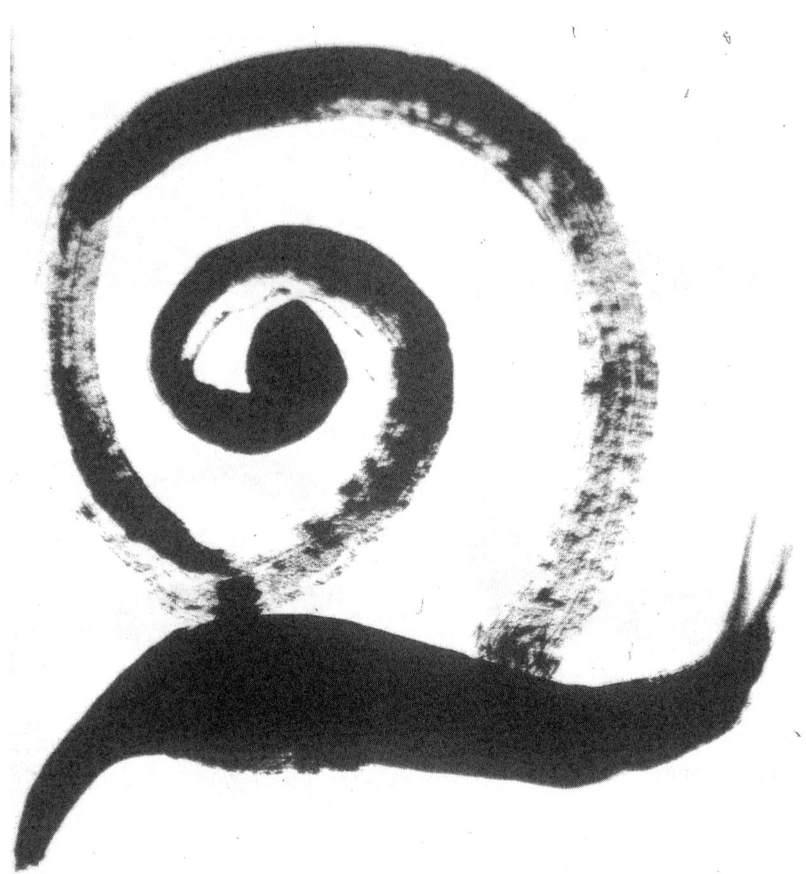

11 Snail Tar Baby One

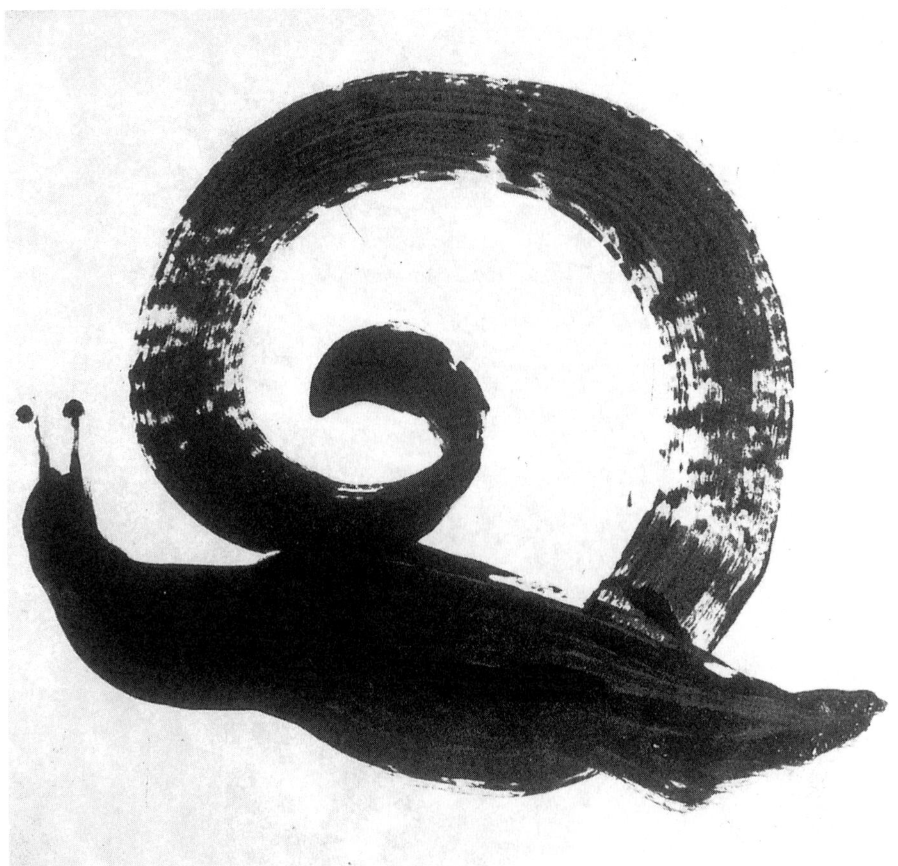

12 Snail Tar Baby Two

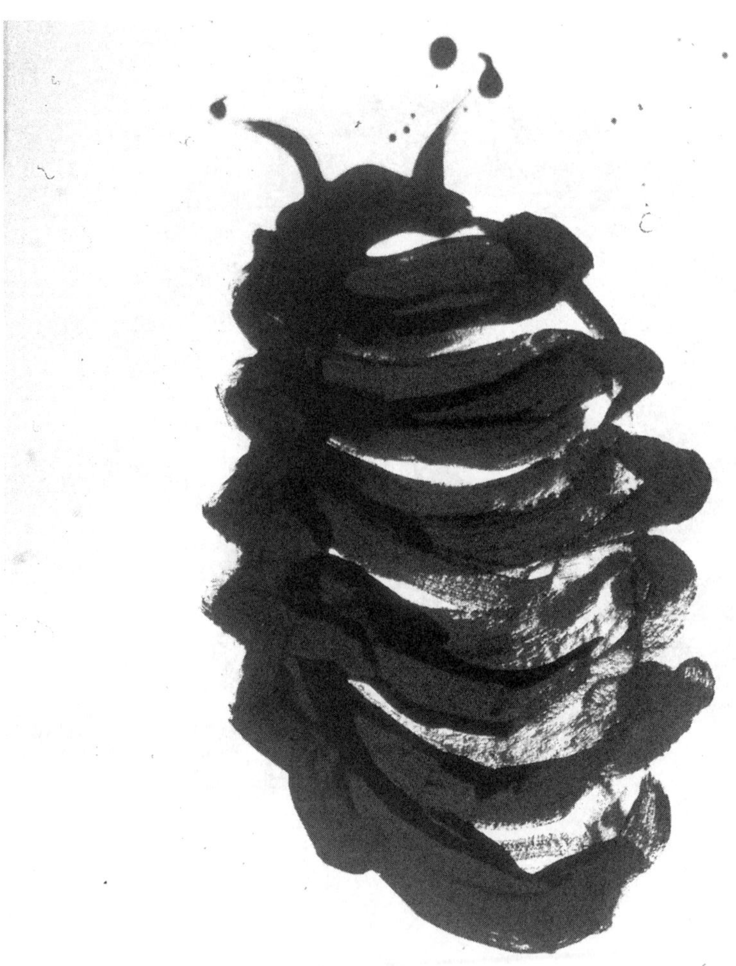

13 Wood Louse Tar Baby

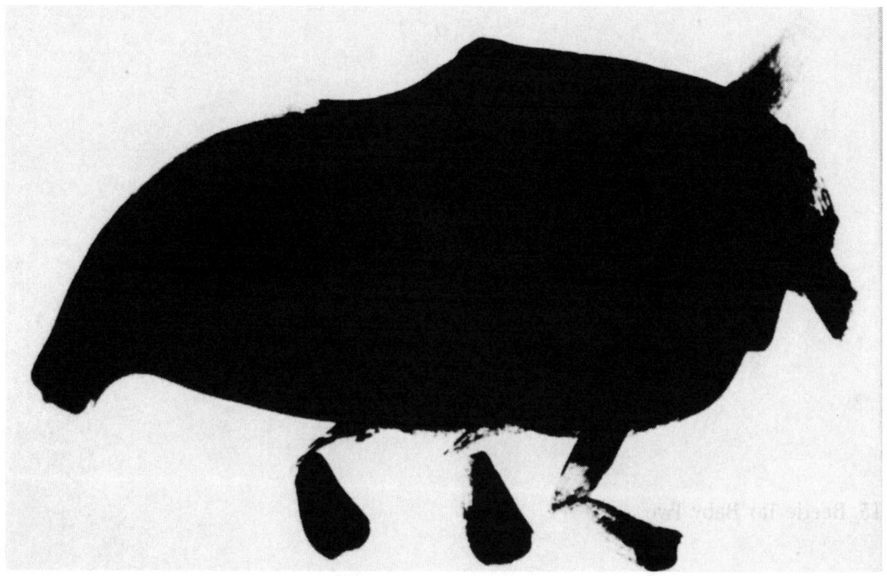

14 Beetle Tar Baby One

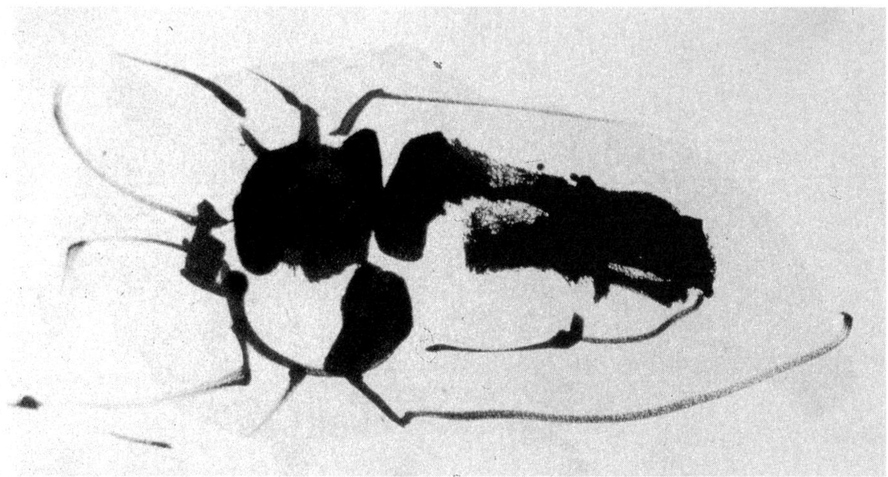

15 Beetle Tar Baby Two

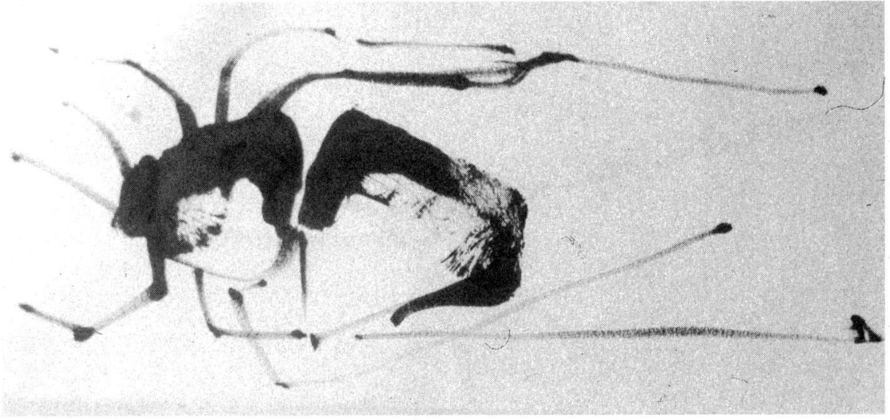

16 Beetle Tar Baby Three

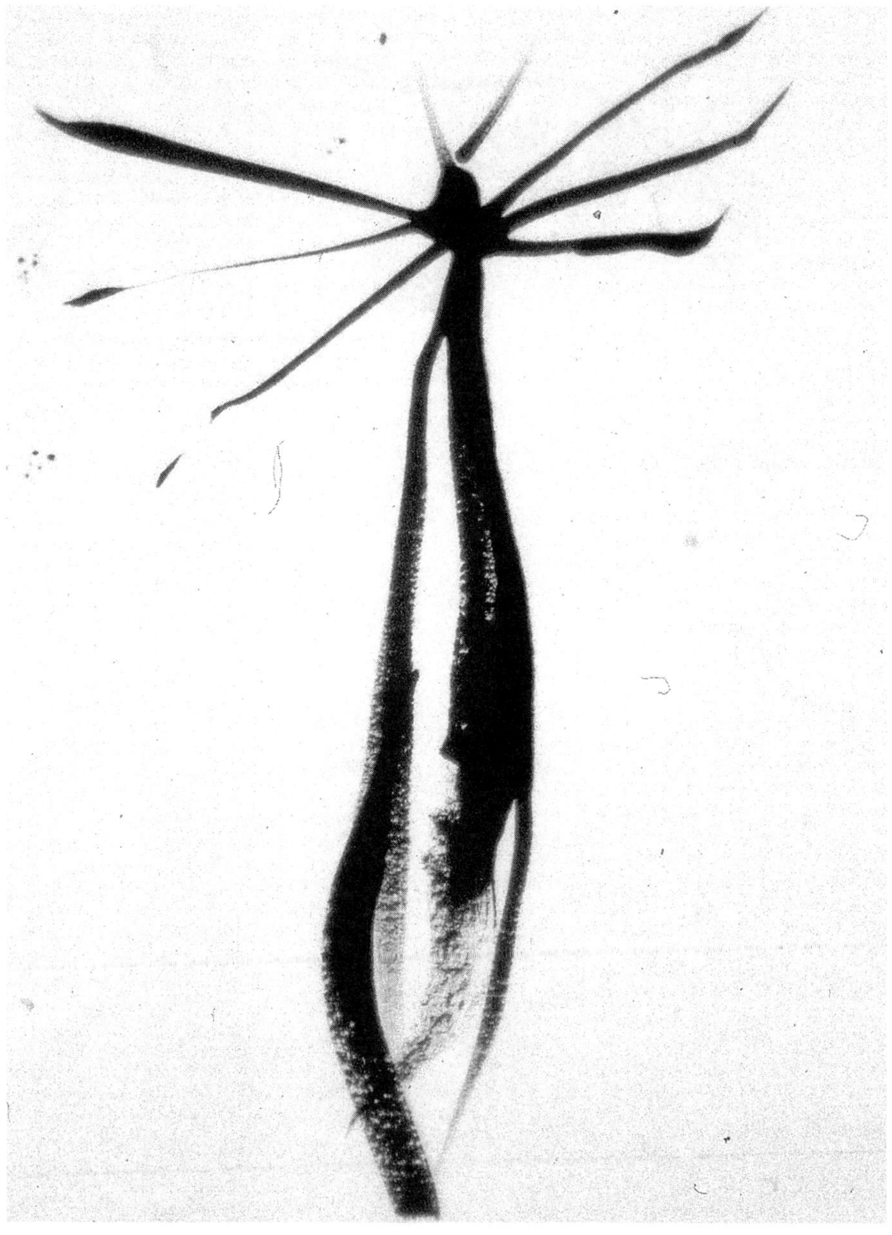

17 Mayfly Tar Baby

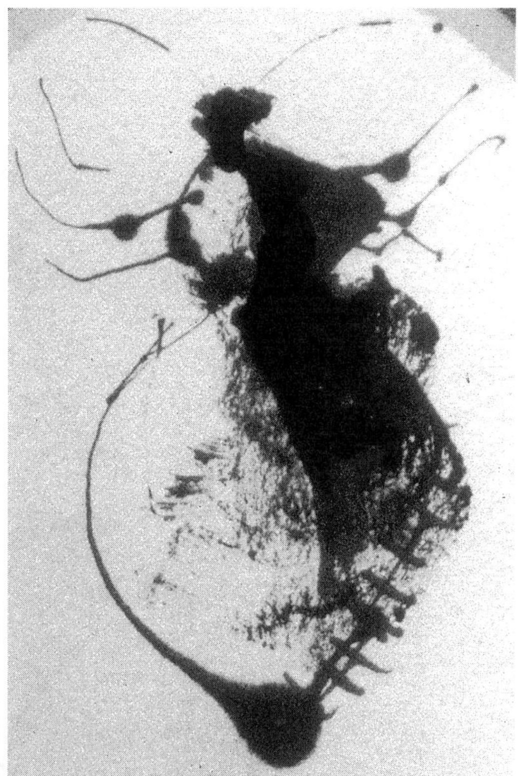

18 Queen Termite Tar Baby

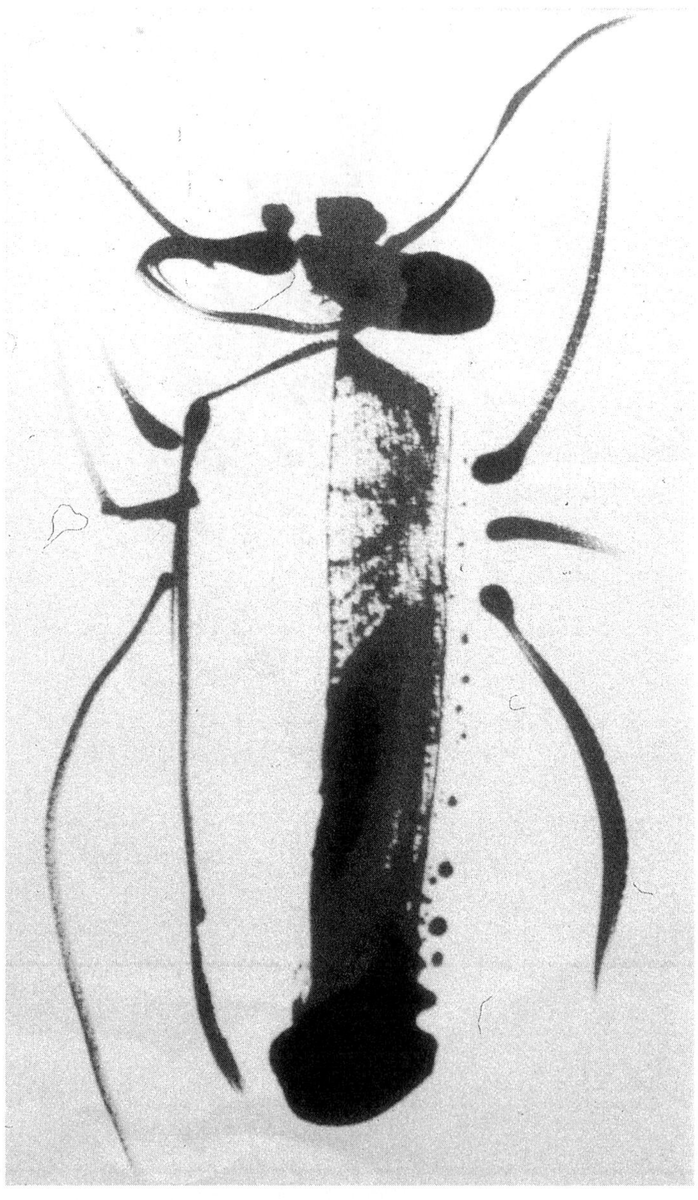

19 Soldier Termite Tar Baby

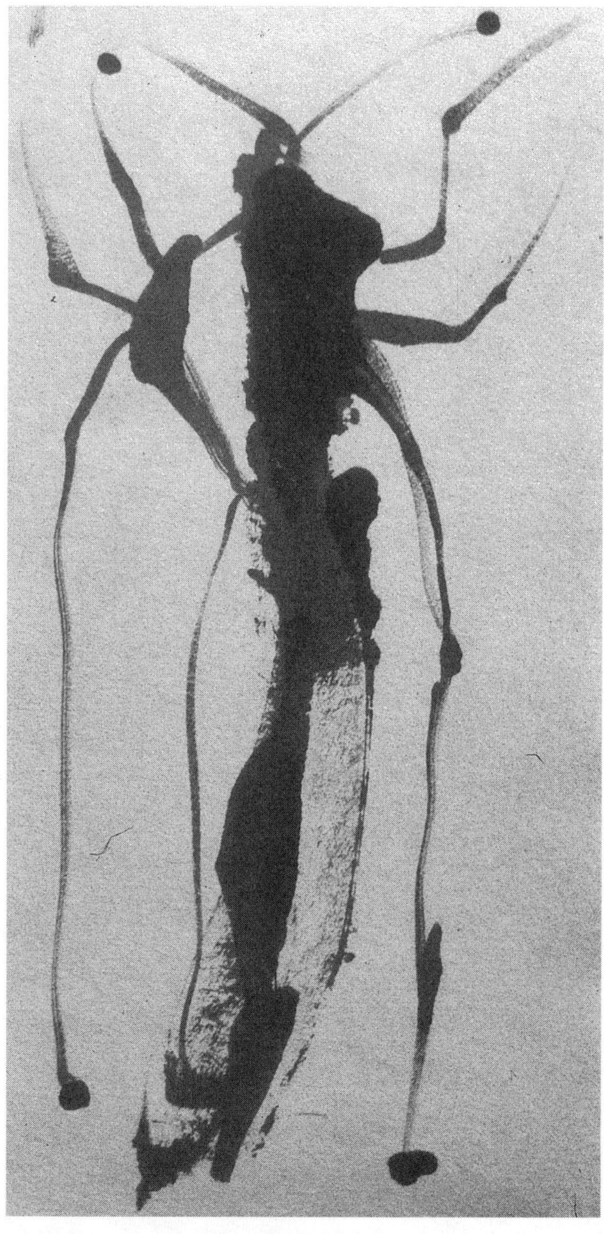

20 Stick Insect Tar Baby One

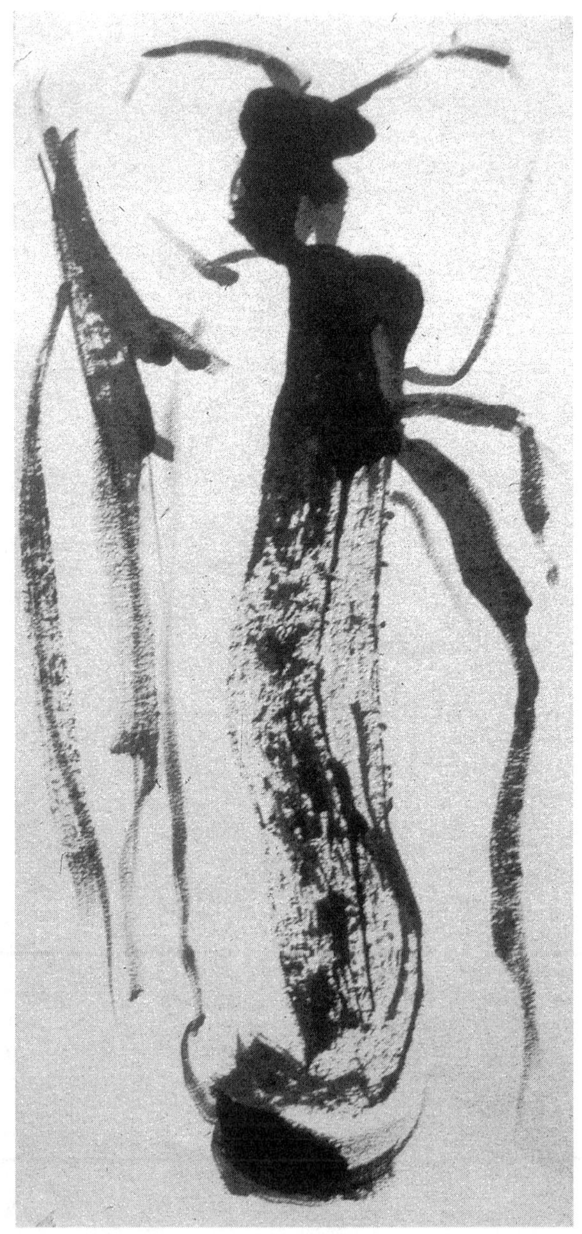

21 Stick Insect Tar Baby Two

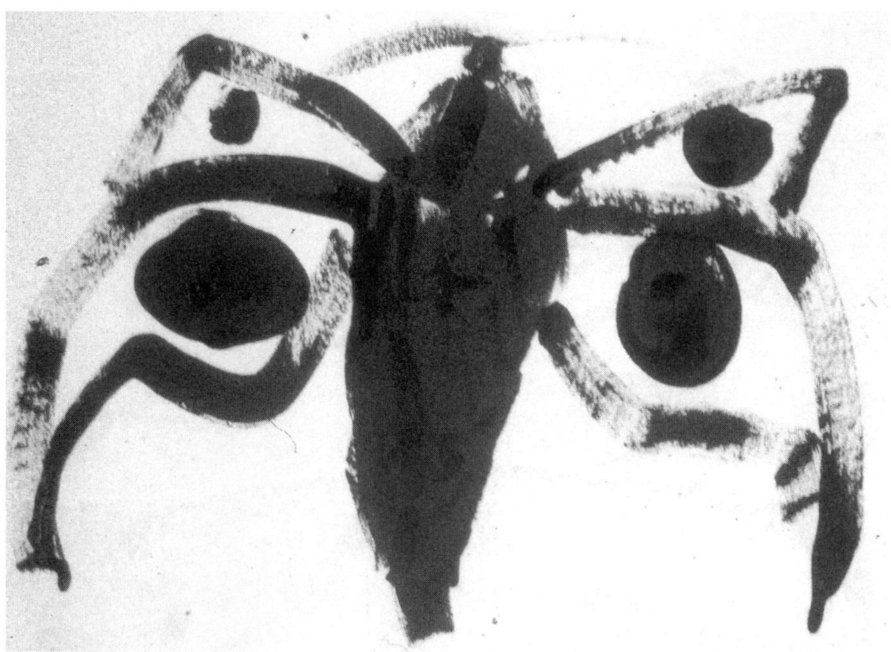

22 Moth Tar Baby

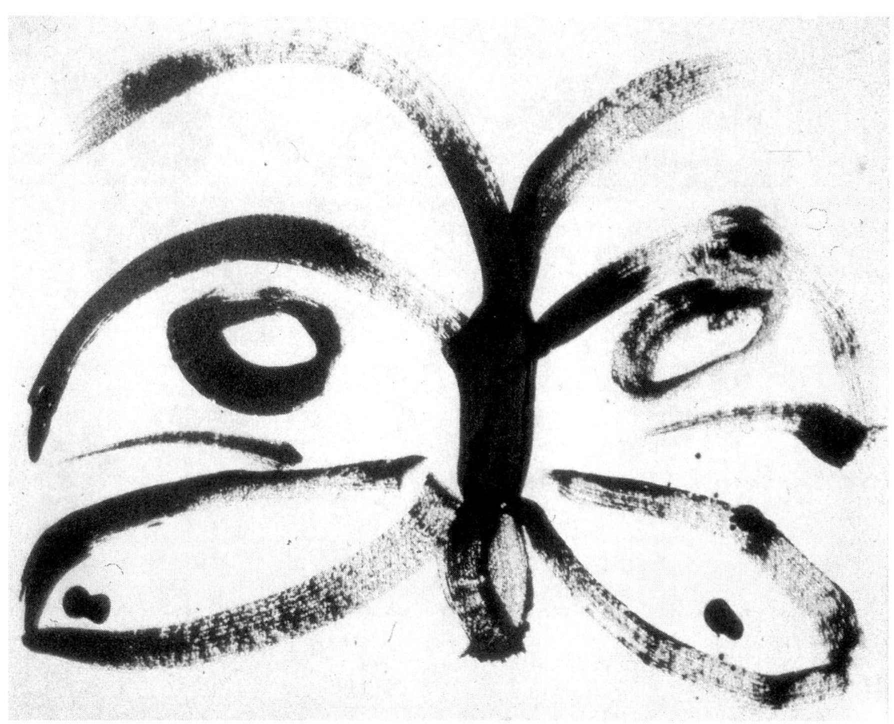

23 Butterfly Tar Baby

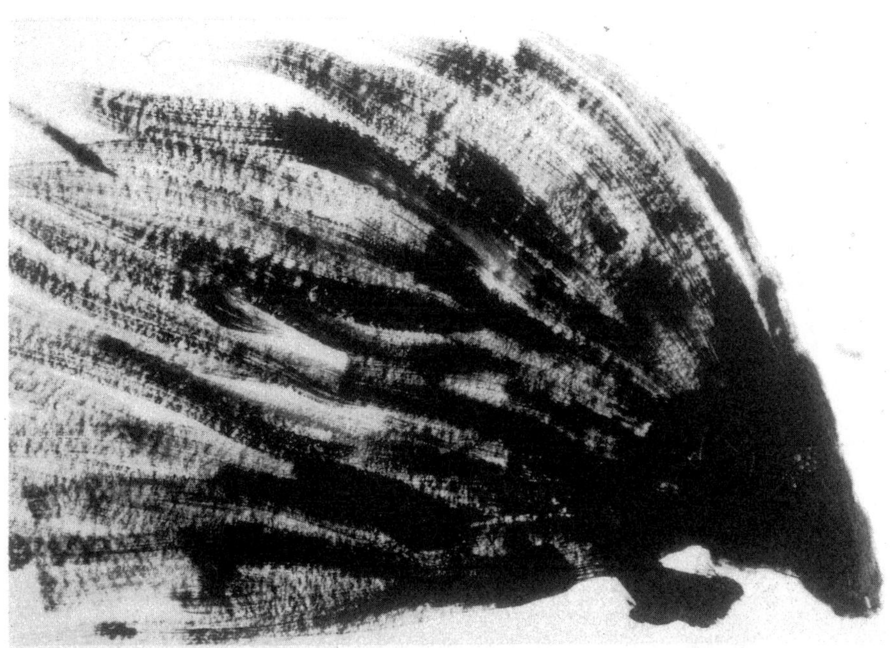

24 Porcupine Tar Baby

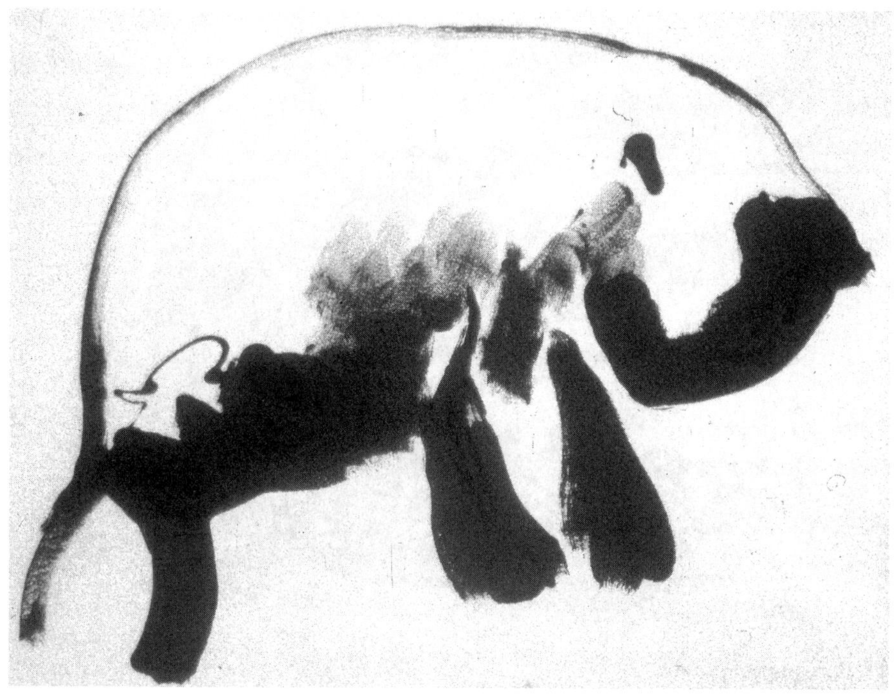

25 Manatee Tar Baby One

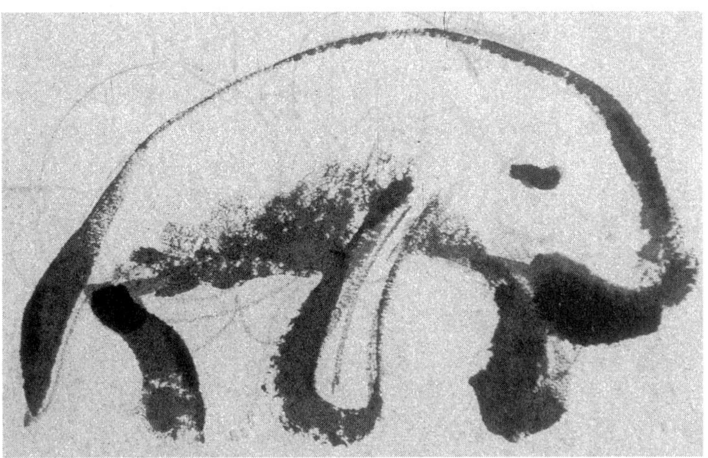

26 Manatee Tar Baby Two

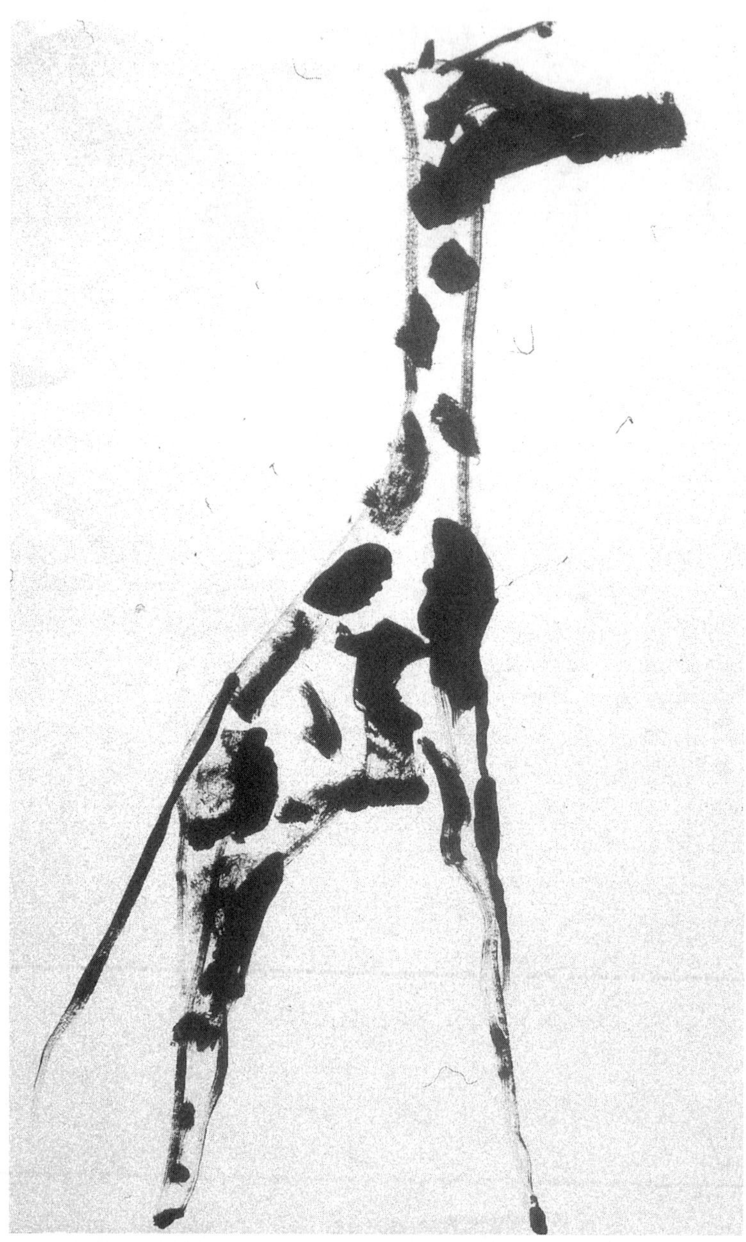

27 Giraffe Tar Baby

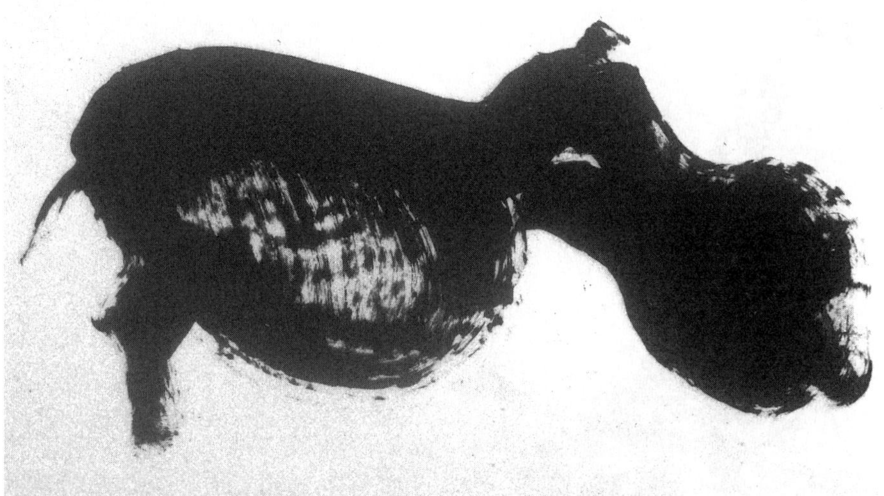

28 Hippopotamus Tar Baby

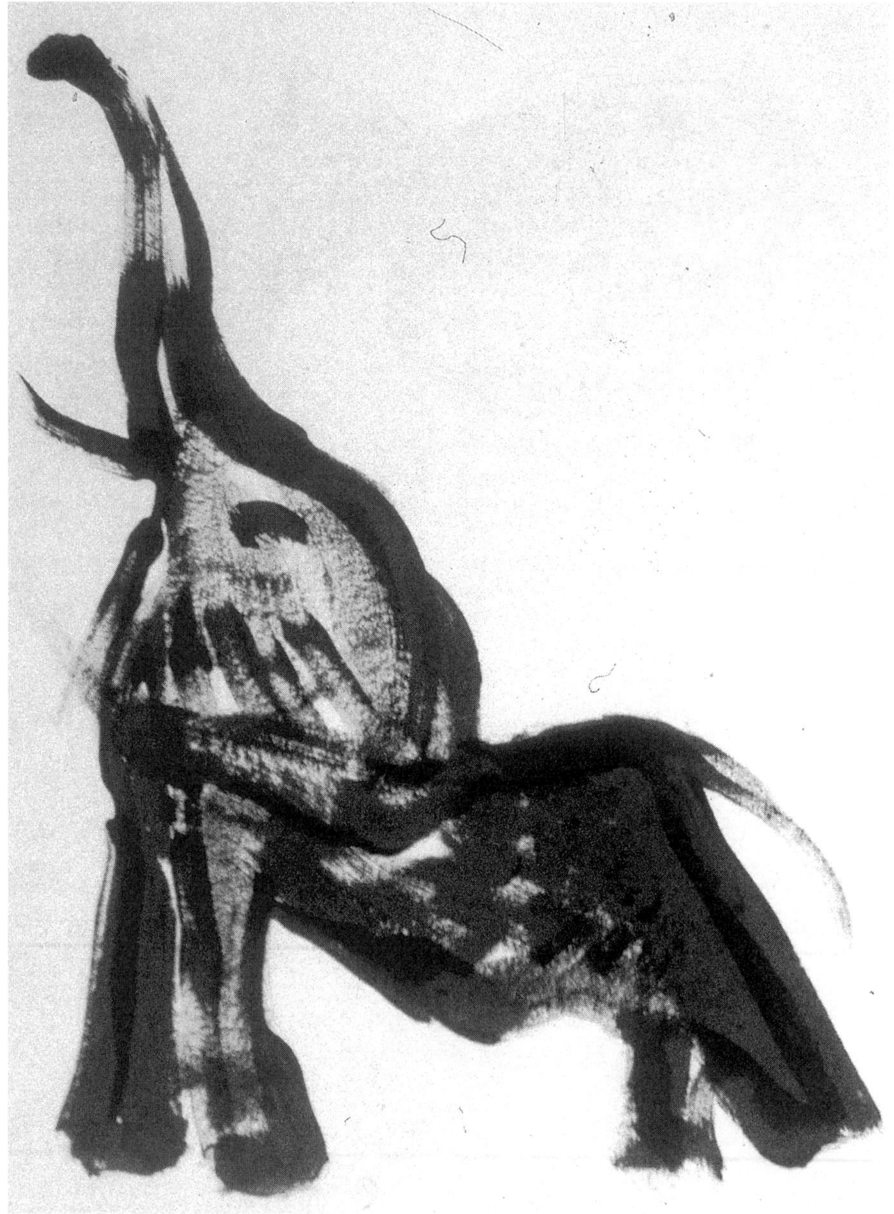

29 Elephant Tar Baby

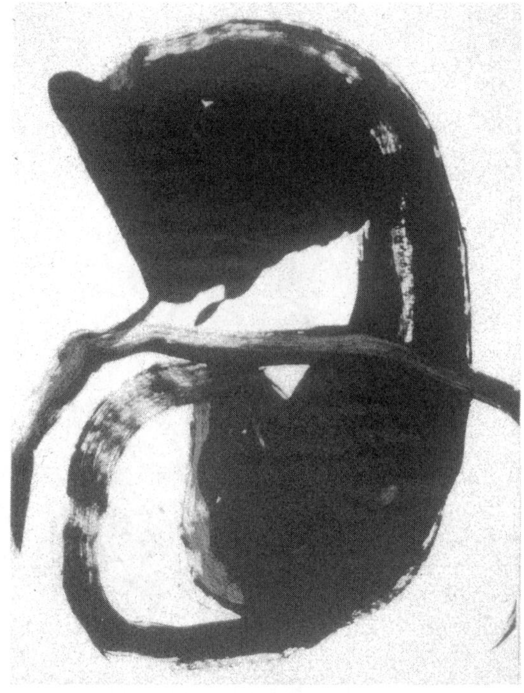

30 Tar Telephone Strangled by its Own Cord One

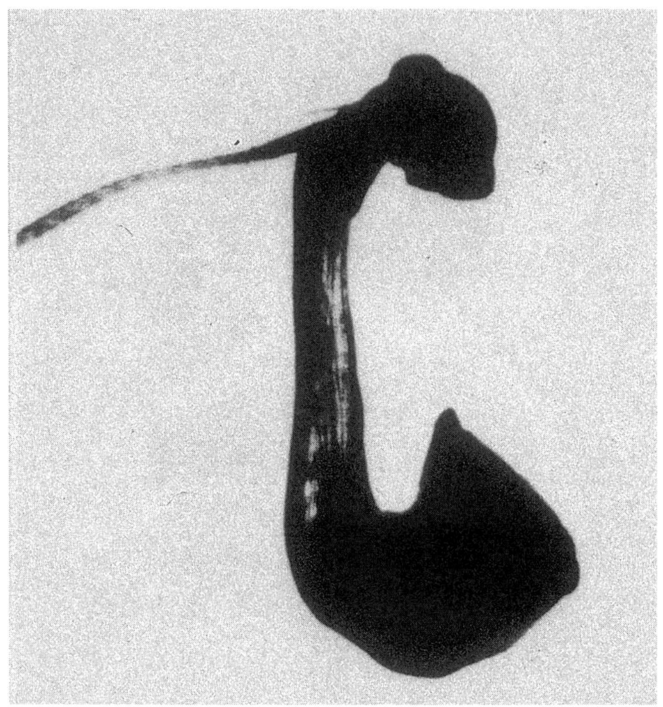

31 Tar Telephone Strangled by its Own Cord Two

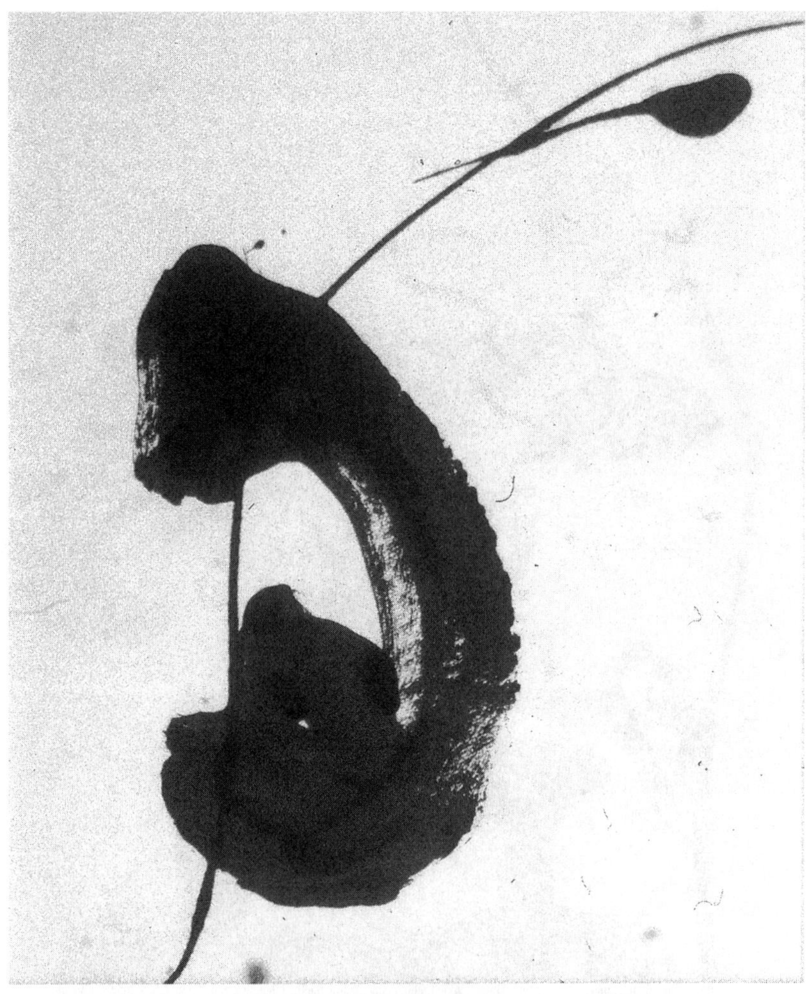

32 Tar Telephone Strangled by its Own Cord Three

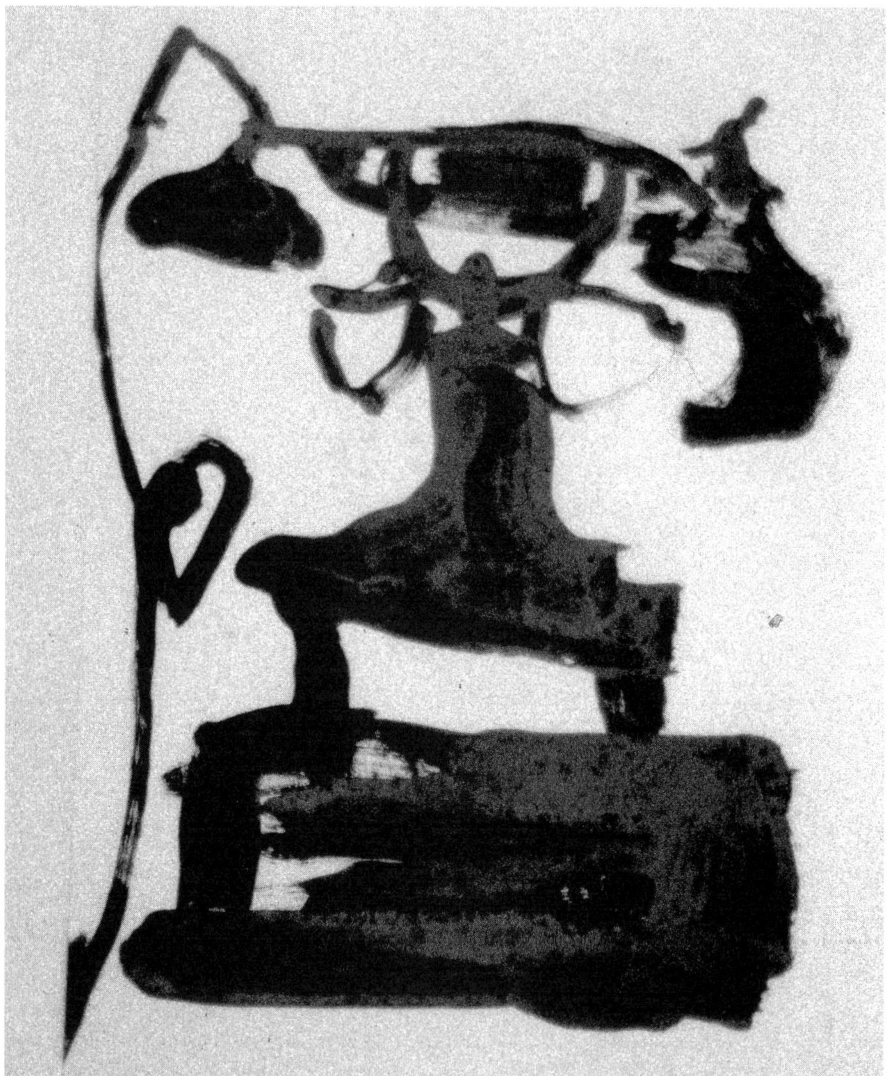

33 Telephone Tar Baby

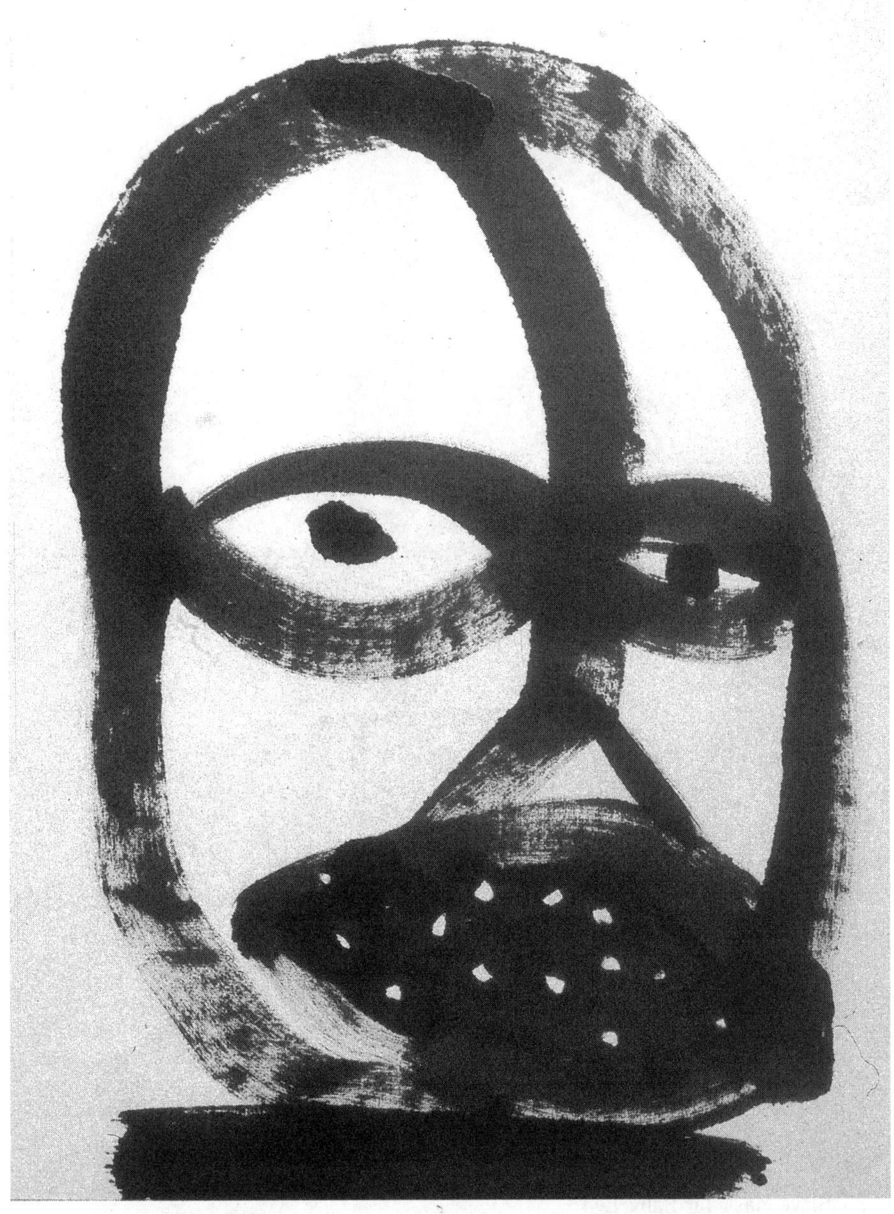

34 Slave Mask Tar Baby One

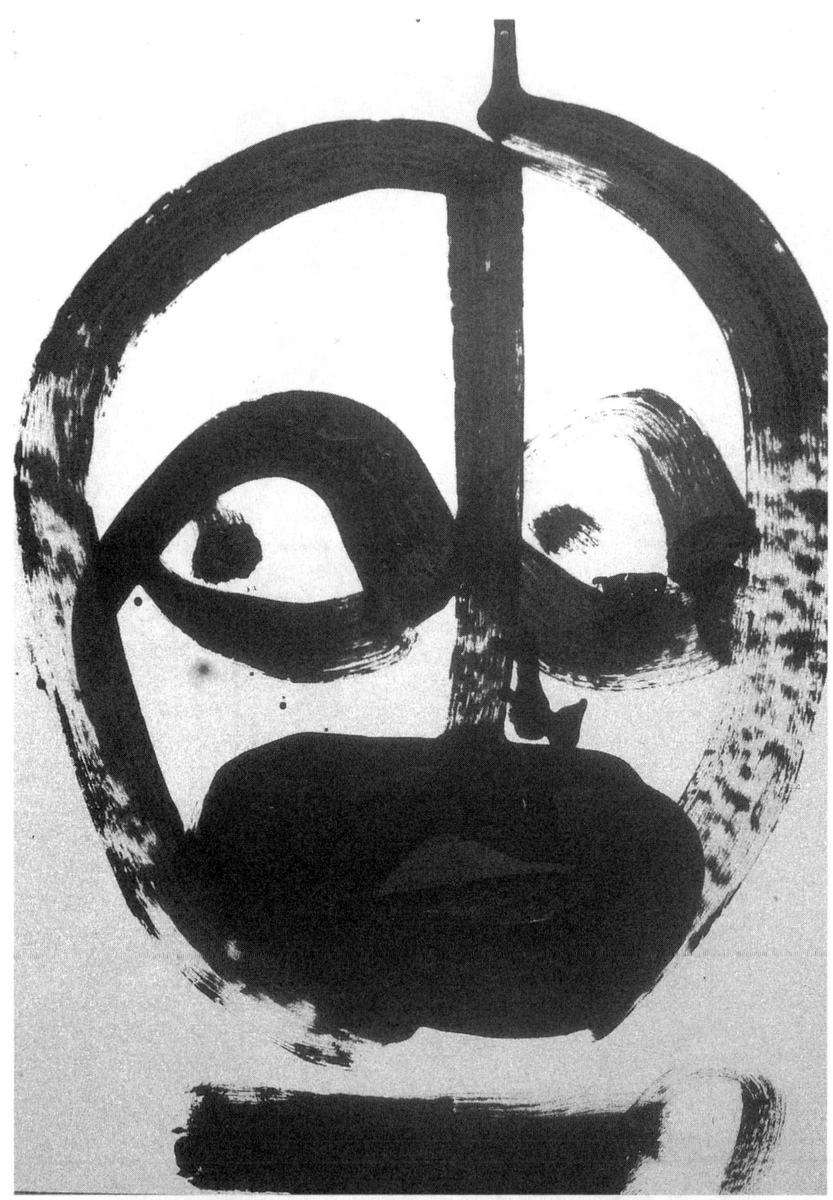

35 Slave Mask Tar Baby Two

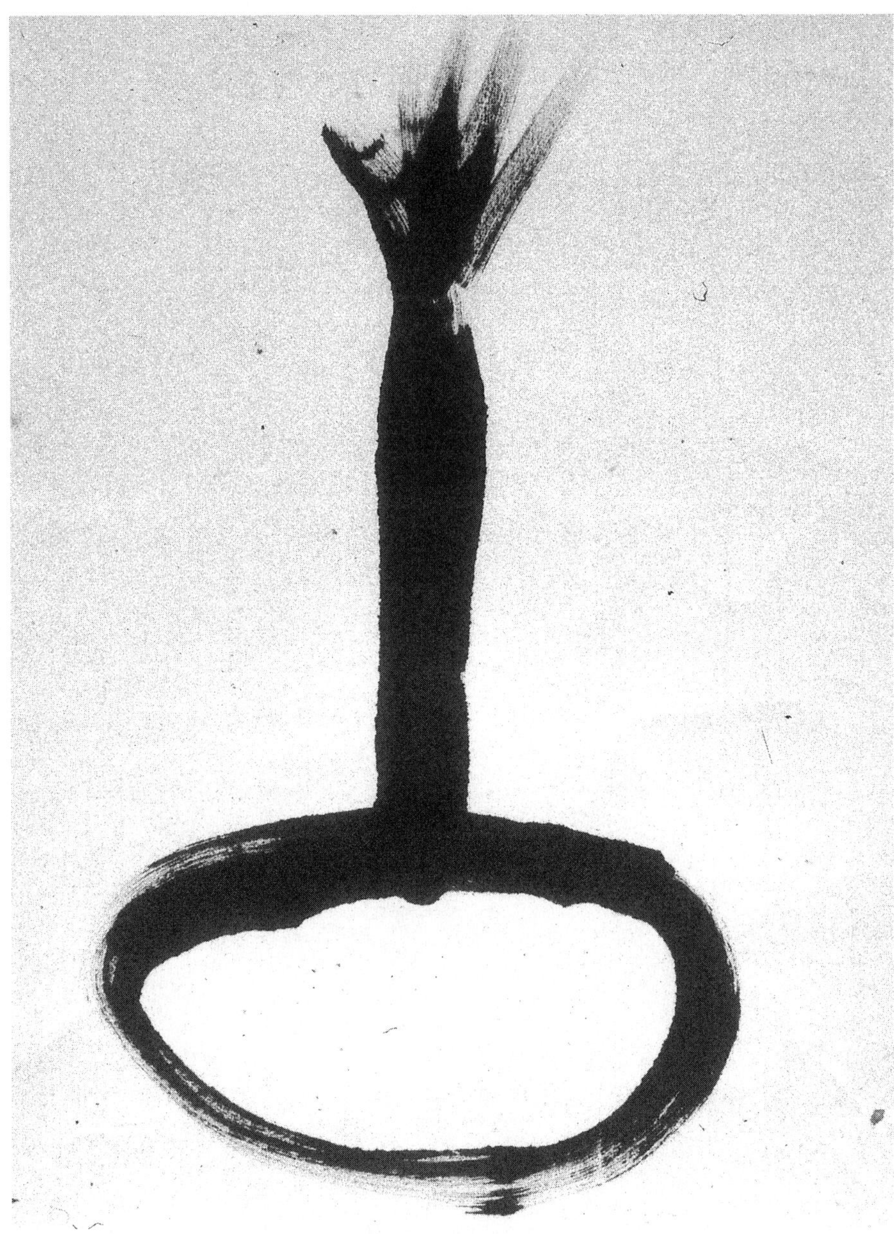

36 Slave Mask Tar Baby Three

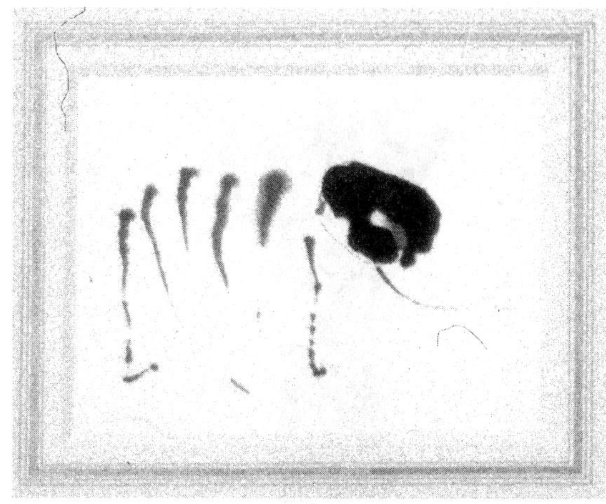

37 Tar Pit Tar Baby

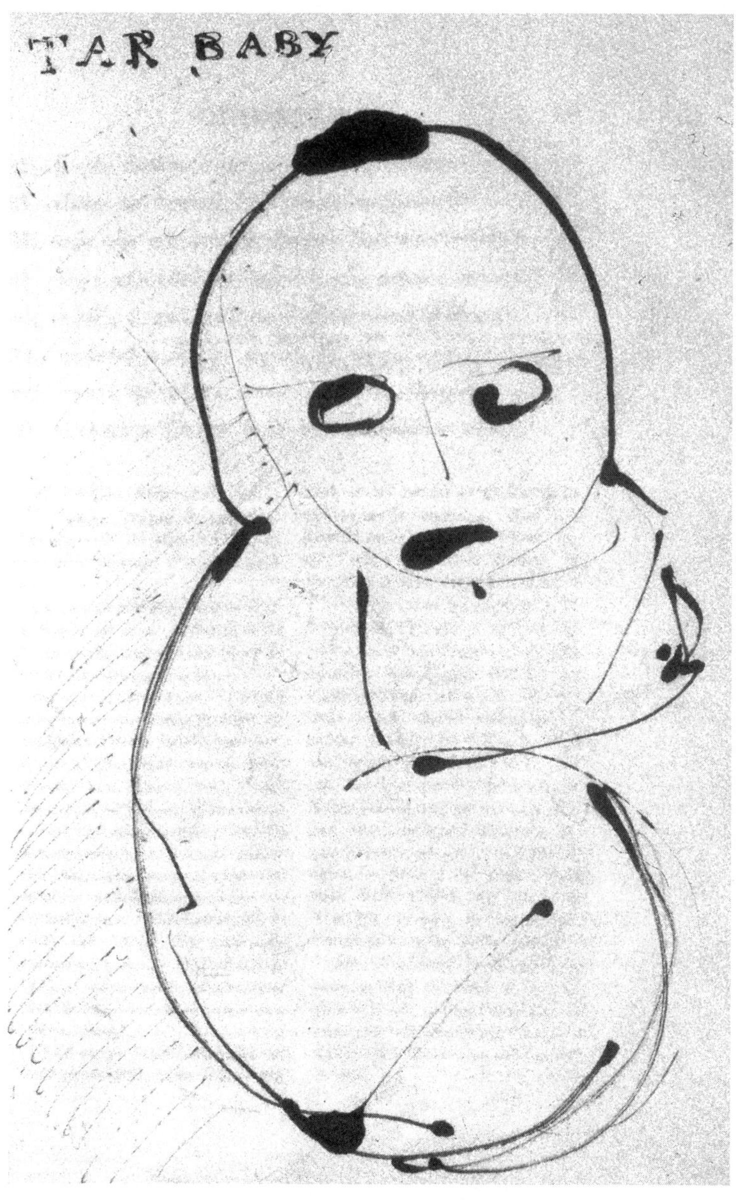

38 Tar Baby Tar Baby

STORIES

TOAST 48
FLIGHT 56
LIGHTS OUT 51
EGYPT 60
A BRUISING ENCOUNTER 64
RUNNING A BATH, HER STORY 68
DOCUMENTED 74
CASTES 81
PLAN 86
NEWTON 89
BOX 91
CINDERS 93
KIDS 95
T POT 96
END OF THE LEG 98
RUNNING A BATH, HIS STORY 101
PICTURE WINDOW 104
NAIL 106
SPADE 108
COLOURS 109
BLACK 117

TOAST

Picture this, a dirty kitchen, in a dirty house, in a dirty street. Up against the wall probably the dirtiest cooker in the world. It's gas, and so caked in grease that it looks more like an animal than a machine. Well it's not just grease, it's all sorts of crazy shit, encrusted, a façade from hell, an illustrated encyclopaedia of junk food, a bad food guide cemetery, a living thing. Inside the oven is a global filth, continents and sub continents had been shuffled together in a supermarket, only to be incarcerated in this peptic safe. Waffles coupled with egg shells, oven chips with frozen peas, half fish fingers penetrating pizza slices, samosas nuzzled up to pasta shells, chicken pies and chicken tika's mingling, different sorts of spaghetti miscegenating like a nest of off-white snakes, and on top of it all a burnt pork sausage stuck up the bum of a jam ring doughnut. Good God, it's a circus, all shapes and sizes, black things, white things and grey, mingle, mingle, mingle you that mingle may, and over all a varnish of chip fat and ketchup. We pull back to see – Marlene and Chester sitting there at an olive green formica table, they are seated on shiny plastic and chrome chairs, with yellow sponge lining poking through rents and tears. They are trying to have a breakfast, waffles and pretend maple syrup.

'The waffles are cold' says Chester.

'Wild Thing won't light' says Marlene.

'Why not?'

'Because its got gunk in it, every damn pore is blocked, is got more shit on its face than a golfer's wife.'

'Well can't you scrape it down, wash it out, or something, give it some surgery with bleach and a bread-knife?'

'Can't you, you lazy sod?'

'No I can't, I've got too much to do?'

'What have you got to do.'

'I've got to think how to warm up these damp cold waffles, now Wild Thing has gone on the blink.'

'It hasn't gone on the blink, it just needs a bit of a hose down.'

The following silence has a loud background noise to it, like a radio not tuned in properly, or like gas coming very fast out of all the burners of a cooker. The silence is punctuated by Chester's frantic search through his dressing gown pockets for his Zippo lighter. He finds it, a huge fiery antique, and flicks it. He turns the wick up to maximum and a two foot flame is soon sending cinder filled smoke up to the ceiling. He takes the waffle, holds it at the apex of the flame, and watches it immediately go soot black and burst into flames. He flings the lighter on the ground, shaking his hand like he has just burned it, which is in fact the case. 'Yowch!' he says, like a cartoon character in pain, 'that Zippo's too hot to

handle.' The silence goes on, until Marlene says:
    'Why don't you do something with that stove now, now that plan B backfired?'
    'I don't know what's backfired there's a bad smell in here, have you farted?'
    Marlene smiles knowingly, and goes on:
    'We're all the same inside, in the same boat, and anyway what was plan A?'
    'Plan A was to give wild thing a clean up.'
    'You do it then, go right ahead.'
    'I can't, the smell of chip fat makes me sneeze, I must have a allergy.'
    'That's one big pork pie, you never had an allergy to chips in your life, you ate a bag of chips last night, and all the batter off of my fish.'
    'That's to miss the point, chips are fine it's the fat that gets me.'
    'That's rich, that's like blaming your hangover on the tonic.'
    'Anyway, it wasn't a bag, it was a parcel, a clean paper parcel, do you remember when they used old newspaper, and how fun it was reading the stories while you ate the chips?'
    'I'm younger than you, I don't remember, I don't think I ever even did that.'
    'Why don't you just get up off your fat arse and get stuck into wild thing, we used to have some kind of a spray thing, a foam, you put on rubber gloves, fire off all this stuff into the oven, and then it does the business, it just eats up everything, turns it into a pulp, a soup, and then you can just mop it up, and there you go, wild thing is as good as new and twice as handsome. Then we can get some waffles.'
    The white noise hiss goes on. The silence is broken by the sound of Chester pushing his chair back, and walking with a surprising brusqueness from the room. Marlene sits there, and we hear sounds off – a terrible fight in the lumber room. Marlene lets out a ripping trump and smiles, at first smiling broadly she then breaks into a half suppressed laugh. Chester comes in carrying a large oil cloth, and asks Marlene what she's laughing at:
    'Nothing, what's in the cloth?'
    'Chirpy, you remember Chirpy, you remember Chirpy don't you, Chirpy has blasted more paint off windows than the IRA. There's a terrible smell in here you know.'
    'O yeah, I remember, Chirpy, he's the man for the waffles.'
    'We need a pin, or a filament or something, to stuff down Chirpy's nozzle, he's kind of gunked up as well.'
    Silence, Marlene pulls a large safety pin with pink enamel head from her lapel, and hands it to Chester. Chester puts the pin in the nozzle and starts moving it rapidly backwards and forwards with a masturbatory alacrity, Marlene looks on quizzically. Chester is working himself into something of lather, when the sweat actually starts running down and off his nose Marlene interjects:
    'Calm down Chester, you'll give yourself a big purple heart attack.'
    'OK OK its got to be clear I've neglected Chirpy, you can't be too careful.'
    'Chester pours from a big can with a nozzle carefully into Chirpy.'
    'What you pouring, Chazzer?'
    'Petrolium.'
    'I thought it was paraffin that Chirpy fed on.'
    'Petrol, it packs more of a punch, and when I've done the waffles, I'm going to introduce chirpy to wild thing. Jesus are you sure you haven't farted there is one terrible stink around here, like bad gas or something.'
    They both look at each other, Marlene picks up a waffle, and holds it out in front of her with her eyes shut like it's a hand grenade with no pin in it. Chester pumps on a small handle on the side of Chirpy with that same wanker's action. We get a good sense of why he is so affectionate about Chirpy. He puts Chirpy down and quick as lightning strikes up Zippo, in a series of quicksilver montage cuts we see – Zippo ignite – the filthy burners on Wild Thing belching out blue flames – Marlene running towards Chirpy screaming no, no, no, no, no – Chester putting Zippo to Chirpy's nozzle – then we pull to outside the terrace of number 64 and see it dissolve into a fireball, while a large silver jet flies over the clear blue sky above the house.

Walking back into the smoking wreckage we see the wrecked black bodies of Chester and Marlene. Wild Thing is burning, sputteringly in the corner, like a candle coming to life, black and gothic against blackened shiny walls, bits of ignited food falling off her sides. We wander over to Chester and Marlene, who lie spread eagled, side by side. We go up and look, slowly up the incinerated bodies, the clothes are tattered, like someone whose been in a comic explosion in a silent film, but this is no joke, just a happy coincidence. We notice the hissing white noise has stopped, and a blackbird is singing outside, while the sound of distant sirens gets stronger. The exposed skin is burned crisp black, in places burned off to reveal completely white cooked flesh beneath. We come to rest with the sight of their two faces, the skin burned off in a perfect set of crisping curls, like the petals on a sunflower, and in the centre of each face a white circle of meat, cooked as white as a chicken breast.

LIGHTS OUT

The train was the last one out, two men stumble in, both a little the worse for wear. Miraculously, the first two seats that they fall into are empty seats, in fact they are double seats and all four are empty, so they fill all four with coats and bags. They do not know each other and nothing much happens. One of them looks intently over his copy of a computer magazine from time to time, he is mid-forties and healthy, though inclining to fat. The train is about to start, with the usual strangely old fashioned whistles and shutting of final barriers. A young woman in a tight black raincoat, real patent leather wrapped around a real sexy figure, crashes through the door, elegantly:

'Peter.'

She says, in a foreign, perhaps South African, accent.

'Thank God I made it.'

She laughs engagingly towards the slightly pudgy man, and she falls with the relaxation of intimacy next to him on the seat. Her face is the colour of a fresh stick of cinnamon, and is framed by elaborate braided locks that fall on the seat like a beaded curtain. The other looks at them both, he is not particularly relevant to this story.

'Peter I'm so sorry, I went to the wrong station, Victoria, not London Bridge, it was sheer luck I made it.'

'Don't worry girl, what if you hadn't, its only a weekend in Amsterdam.'

'Don't pretend Peter, you know we've both been dying for this.'

'Oh for God's sake, you're here now, lets shut up and enjoy it.'

'So you're pissed off with me, you got worried, enough stress for one week, hey?'

'Don't worry girl, I'm not going to say it again.'

There is a fairly prolonged silence during which a black train guard, with an absurdly fat and large trolley of sandwiches, drinks, chocolates and various less immediately identifiable eatables, manoeuvres his way down the train. He apologises with great volume each time he strikes the pent up, penned in, pin-striped knee, or tightly knotted, lightly tighted knee of some resigned not quite designer commuter. They know he is doing his best in an impossible situation, he knows that these hard, desperate, fragile people are on a hair trigger, and if he as much as grazes one of them, with intent, he will be, in terms of his employment, knackered. Peter breaks the silence:

'Well, so you're going to show us a good time Hendricke?'

'I'll show you the real Amsterdam, my home town.'

'You should work in tourism.'

'I do, in a way, you're definitely seeing the best side of Holland.'

'I'm definitely seeing the backside of Holland.'

They laugh suggestively and fall into a passionate clinch, like some kind of nineteen-fifties teen couple, not the kind of thing you usually expect from people this age in these clothes on the 11.20-from-London-to-somewhere-very-rich. They carry on snogging old time for about twenty minutes. Then the train stops and she leaps up, elegantly, gets out, elegantly, blows a kiss through the window, elegantly, and disappears enticingly, like Mata Hari, into the night, turning once to mouth three words the first of which is Airport.

The train moves out, and the other man, smiling in open admiration, says thickly:
'That's some woman.'
Peter, wiping the lipstick from his mouth, and chops, replies, fuzzily:
'She's Dutch, from Amsterdam.'
'So what do you call that, is she an Amsterdamstresse.'
'Jesus I don't know, but she's good fun.'
'Well I hope you have a good holiday.'
'It's no holiday, I'll tell you.'
'It sounded like she thought it was.'
'She knows the score, it's a working weekend, and for her it's a lot of work, we don't speak one word of Dutch.'
'Well who's we?'
The conversation is halted as the drinks trolley begins its slow progress into the compartment passage beyond their suddenly tortured forms. They have the seat near the corridor where the trolley makes its most extreme and delicate manoeuvres. Waiting till the trolley has just disappeared Peter roars:
'Hey Guard, some drinks!'
The guard reappears and Pete says, looking at his new friend:
'One for the road.'
Then without waiting, or looking, for a reply he replies:
'All your gins and all your tonics, and one for yourself Mein Herr.'
The black waiter has just re-arrived, he unloads eight miniature bottles of Gin and six miniature cans of tonic onto the table, collects the notes, and moves on. As the conversation progresses Pete and his new mate get through the drinks pronto.

'You want to know who's we, well we's a team, a special kind of a hockey team, the London to somewhere rich, fuckrich financial consultant hockey team, off for a weakent with our Dutch soul mates. We don't speak a word of Dutch, and we won't be seeing them after the game, not if we can help it. So we need an interpreter, and my sweet friend Hendricke is the man for the job, in fact she's a man for all seasons.'
'So how much money do you make?'
'Look don't ask all the questions, how much money do *you* make?'
'Twenty grand a year, before tax.'
'Got any education?'
'I've got two degrees and was in full time education till I was twenty six.'
Peter sits back and visibly swells, it's like he's just been given the elixir of life, he composes himself before enjoying the descent into the real Pete which follows:
'Well I've got no fucking degrees, and I'm not twenty six, but I make one hundred and fifty grand a year, after tax, in a bad year. And that's an education I'm giving you, what do you do you poor sod?'
The other is not insulted, but really impressed, this is, after all, real money talking to him:
'I wanted to work in a university, now I am a schoolteacher.'
'Well that's nice, you did a good thing, you won't be teaching my kids, not on that kind of a fucking charity handout, but education is a good thing, no mistake about it.'
'So what do you do with it all, all that money.'
'That's not real money, that's not anything but pocket money, the boss makes the real money, the bitch, she makes as much as I make five times over just in bonuses.'
'So what motivates you people?'

'Look, I have a good life, I want a better life, I love my kids, I love my house, I love my people and I love my country, and not necessarily in that order.'

'You really love your country that's nice, would you die for your country?'

Pete, visibly, moved goes on:

'I would go to war, I would fight for, I would die, I would gladly die, for my country, my country has made me what I am.'

The train pulls up and the conversation comes to a premature end. These two people seem to be striking up an unusual intimacy for this part of the world and it is exciting to them both, but Pete must exit. He stumbles off the train, and lurches out at the ticket barrier, he hails a shining black cab.

II

The cab pulls up outside a large mock-Tudor dwelling set well back, on a curvy leafy road. Pete walks, arrow straight, down the path to the front door, then checks, with a cunning look in his eye, as he sees a light on in an upstairs window. He moves with surprising and simian smoothness across the lawns to a gigantic shed full of every form of garden equipment. After the customary false starts and cursing he wrestles with a huge extendable ladder. He then charges, ladder in hand and head down, across the grass back to the house. He silently pulls out one telescoping extension, and props the ladder up against the wall, and then climbs with familiar smoothness to the top.

Through the window his view is seriously restricted by heavy curtains, and dim light, but unmistakably he sees a pair of white buttocks rhythmically penetrated by a tall, naked and highly athletic young black man. He can also make out a young, slender, white arm and wrist which gently strokes the outside of the black thigh nearest to Pete's view. He screws his eyes tight shut and descends the ladder in this self imposed state of blindness. He walks purposefully to the front door, and makes one hell of a racket getting his keys out and into the lock, then he bangs the door shut, as if a cyclone is behind him. Then he goes to the kitchen, picks up a remote control and puts on the sound system. A desperate black voice as deep as the ghetto chants, again and again, to the rhythm of a window rattling base:

'Hey nigger is you deaf, is this the final solution?'

He picks up the remote control again and we move over to the sound of *Death and the Maiden*.

He pours himself a large single malt whiskey and sits down gingerly.

The sound of bounding, softly clad feet leads into the appearance of three youngsters, Georgina, Sebastienne and Dominic.

'Yo, dad, you're back early, we thought you were out late for a piss up at the factory.'

Says Sebastienne.

'Yeah, I left early, I've got Amsterdam early tomorrow.'

'Nice one.'

Says George.

'I've never been to Amsterdam.'

Says Dominic.

'You'll get there, I'll bet on it.'

Says Pete, and adds with only the faintest trace of side to his voice:

'You're all OK are you, having fun?'

Without so much as a second thought Sebastienne comes out with:

'I don't know about Dominic, he's been playing in the attic, but we've been having a great time, watching this neat video, a sort of parents from hell revenge horror flick.'

Pete has to admire his son's cool. Kids these days, they're just ready for the real world, but Pete isn't finished yet, he rises to the occasion, and is pleased with the way he meets this bold faced lie:

'Well leave it in the machine for me will you, I need a pick-me-up.'

Everyone laughs in an unnervingly spontaneous way. Then George goes on:

'You bet dad, can we borrow the Audi to take Dominic to meet his friend, he's this wicked DJ, and he's only on tonight?'

'Go ahead.'

Says Pete wearily, giving up the game for now. The door slams and Pete pours himself another whiskey and takes some small white pill or other. He whips out his midget sized super slim mobile and delicately picks out a number:

'Hi, Jardine, hi. Sorry to phone at this time, but I think there might be a problem… no, not work, you know I wouldn't do that to you… yeah, how did you guess, it's about the kids and your Dominic in particular… look, I can't put this delicately, I'll just have to call a spade a spade, I think he's having sex with one of them, but I don't know which one… how do I *know*, Jardine trust me I *know*… all right I'll tell you… now I got home early to go to Amsterdam… yeah, yeah, I'll send your love to Hendricke… and the attic light was on… yes that is strange, look let me just get through with this… OK… now no one goes in the attic, it's a spare bedroom we never use, so I imagine its like a robbery, so I climb up a ladder… yeah I know it sounds like Fawlty Towers Jardine but this is deadly serious… yeah I know what I'm saying… and I can only see a bit of what's going on but I sure as hell saw your Dominic buggering something white… look don't say that, the fact they were white isn't here or there… I knew you'd start this, look just trust me colour is not important here, just the facts… how do I know it was… no it wasn't a party, they are completely on their own… look it's one of them, although I couldn't be sure in that light if it was a seventeen year old boy or a fifteen year old girl… no no mistake, for Christ sake there's no one else in the house… look I'm not being heavy I just want to set out the options… give me a chance hey, calm down, just listen… yes I know what you went through to adopt Dominic… yeah he's a tribute to you… but there's a problem… now if it's the former it's cool, he may be my son but he's got his own life to lead his own way but if it's George, we're on thin ice… no Jardine it's nothing to do with that… No, just look, Dominic could be in deep shit, it's the law Jardine… now don't you fall apart on me… yeah I know it's been a heavy week… yes, I know how much you need to keep the stress areas of your life clinically separated… I'm tired too, we've got to think it through… what are we going to do about this… OK… good point, how do I verify… yeah I know they are not morons… yeah I know they'd deny everything… yeah they already have, in so many words… look they've already come down in all their bloody clown costumes and trainers and stuff… no, OK, ok their clothes are their business…but look they lied straight in my face and looked right through me, and headed for some dance hall thing… so you're saying there is absolutely nothing we can do… not a leg to stand on… Jesus, I know it wouldn't stand up in a court of law… I know the Police have bigger fish to fry… no there were no drugs involved, maybe a couple of beers… Jardine, is this relevant to the point in hand… I realise she could still technically be a virgin, so what… Oh Jesus Jardine, how do you know all this stuff, you are damn hard… no really, is that really what they're into… yeah I know it's more fun for the boys… what about George she's only fifteen… she's my responsibility, you know what I went through to get custody… what did you say… I can't believe you said that… no I don't believe that white women want to be hurt… look I don't think we are getting anywhere… no, it's just I can't handle this kind of fantasy stuff right now… OK we'll talk tomorrow.'

He puts the fine little phone on the big white table and sits down and looks wearily at the stairs. He climbs five flights of his Banker's Gothic mansion until he gets to the attic. The bed has been untidily made, he pulls back the sheets, they are spotless white, he examines the pillows, sniffing like a gun dog and rubbing like a dry cleaner, they are as pure as new fallen snow. He sighs and lies down. He looks at the ceiling, screws up his face, clenches his fists, leaps up, picks up a goose down pillow and hurls it with all his strength at the towering, custom-built wardrobe opposite him, runs full tilt after the pillow and bangs his head violently into the spot where it hit. An upper door falls open with a click, and a white blow up doll falls vertically, elegantly, down, he catches her lightly, like a dancing partner, and lays her gently on the bed. He lies down beside her, groans with a sound like tearing paper, and drops into the land of nod.

III

His dream is as follows. Georgina, Sebastienne and Dominic lead him to the glossy gold tipped black railings outside his house. Dominic takes out a pair of smart silver handcuffs and they fasten him to the railings. George picks up one of those spotless goose down pillows and cuts it open with scissors. Sesastienne appears from nowhere with an enormous smoking chrome bucket full of roofing tar, with George and Dominic's help, they upend it over Pete. When the smooth blackness first slides over him he moves his arms and legs like an exhausted swimmer about to go down, and breathes the same way too, but then almost immediately he screams and screams, but his screams are muffled by handfuls of feathers being stuffed in his mouth. There are clouds of feathers everywhere, and he peers through them at the looming faces of the young people. They do not laugh, they just look curious. The feathers have now stuck to him, he beats his wings and soars heavenwards, in a very dream-like way the handcuffs are no longer part of the picture. As he ascends he passes a window, and there, lying on the bed in the attic, is the beautiful Hendricke, he flies in through the window. What a surprise.

FLIGHT

The sun, rising in the sky, poured a rain of fire on to the coast.

Maupassant, "Idyll"

It was a bad scene, the third day that flights had been cancelled out of São Paulo. The signs had been good, they always are if you ask anyone with a microphone, or access to a microphone. In Brazil, there are no signs, just the assurance of everything going quite right. Maybe that's the most dangerous sign.

It had been as a result of such reassurance that they had initially decided against even thinking about the flight, but then a real human being had answered the phone. Dominic had made the call and the voice had told him quite realistically that there was no chance of a flight, no chance at all, that money, position, and the rest of it was irrelevant. When pushed the official had gone on almost hysterically, and said that he, the speaker, and he, the spoken to, knew what this meant, within Brazil. There was no chance, no chance at all, politics. Then the phone went down. That was all it took. Dominic, who had been around a bit, in South London, and even Central America, decided that, despite the fact that he and his delighted and newly delivered wife, were quite happy, by mutual consent, to remain in the lovely villa they had rented in Ouro Preto, something was up. Dominic had been around enough to know that no-one, no man, behind a microphone, in an airport, in Brazil, spoke to first class passengers that way. It was beyond the pale, unimaginable, there had to be an explanation, and it had to be that there were tickets galore, and that this official was running scared, and had some pretty fatty deals to hide.

Dominic worked all this out in a tick, under no other circumstances could he have made the decision to send his wife off to that god forsaken airport, breast-feeding a beautiful girl only two months old. But he was not impetuous, and he stood back, in his mind, just to double check. A two day airport strike, two hours of mobile phone assurance that the strike was over, assurance from the highest quarters. Followed by a call to book a first class ticket and an official who stated the total impossibility of gaining any such thing. The formula was perfect, a clean flight through. When he phoned back he got, as expected, a very different reaction, the routine sounds of a young woman who was utterly confident that the whole thing would be fine, that all the flights in the world could only be running on time, for all first class passengers. Under normal circumstances that would have terrified him to death, set off the flashing lights, but under Brazilian protocol at this level nothing could be more reassuring. Only minutes before he had heard the life insurance of a genuinely antagonistic and negative male in a position of some authority, who had warned him off in absolute terms. Dominic positively smiled as he put down the phone and thought about the levels at which one had to deal with the international complexities of airport cultural interchange, in what it was still right to call the Third World.

He marched through to the mezzanine bar, waved away the maid, took his favourite stool, carved in the form of a parrot, and poured a beer. He then shouted out:

'George, we're home and dry.'

There was no reply:

'George and Mathilda we are home and dry.'

He repeated. He put down his beer and walked down the stairs to the first floor and along the first floor to the beautiful, and pricelessly illegal brazil-wood staircase. He walked to the bedroom, and recollecting his selfish impetuosity he whispered, in what he considered an enticing tone:

'We are home and dry.'

When there was no answer at the door he shout-whispered through the door:

'The ticket is signed, sealed and delivered, you will return for Easter.'

Still no sound, so he pushed the door open gently, and tiptoed in, with a painfully swaying gate. His wife, whey and grey faced lay with the little girl, who looked hopelessly done in as well. Both were asleep on a pillow, staring out beneath their shut eyes. Even in sleep the little girl seemed to express an infinite sourness towards her mother's exposed breast and flat nipple.

He did not know what to do, he picked up a strange whistle, with parrot feathers all over it, which no one had been able to operate since he bought it a week ago, and then he blew into it. An indescribable sound came out, like a cat's voice, amplified, when the cat had been thrown into a vat of boiling fat. That woke the infant and mother. The mother roared, in a terrible lamentation, the child went white, then blue, and began to try to make human sounds. These small whisperings came very high in the catalogue of unregistered human misery.

Consternation all round, mutual recrimination, the recovery of normal consciousness, all except for Mathilda. Mathilda howled like some small animal that was being gradually deprived of the means of life. Luckily Dominic had his wife's ear at this point and they managed to exchange the somewhat urgent details. The plane was all set to go off at eleven nine local time. Two first class tickets had been booked, one for George, one for Mathilda, and Dominic was staying, as he needed to, to polish off a little of this and that. He would follow on in exactly eighteen hours time. The Mercedes would call in two hours to the minute. There was no time for debate, and as far as George was concerned why should there be, Dominic was always reliable, if not always sensitive to all her needs. In less than twenty-two hours she would be home, in the home counties, and so would Mathilda.

The car was gorgeous, as always, and the air conditioning superb. George, with perhaps too much European sensitivity, or perhaps a continued delight in the extent to which she could in this country, demand and command, softly, told the driver, through his microphone, that he should put down the blind between the driver's compartment and hers before she began feeding her baby. He instantly obliged and the dark glass curtain slowly descended. She placed her fat, small, white, breast and her engorged nipple near the baby's little mouth, it would not feed, it had not fed well since they arrived in Brazil. Maybe it did not like the heat, in any case it had not fed very much since it was born. George stared at the love of her life, Mathilda, and worried, and put the nipple near Mathilda's mouth, and in her mouth, it made no difference. Poor little Mathilda, she *would* sleep, and more worryingly she would not feed. The car slowed suddenly and the bright advertising boards and the fluorescent barriers and check point kiosks started up the ritual of entering the airport. The car slowed to a crawl, George pulled up the feeding bra which she had optimistically kept undone throughout the journey. She put the week little thing in its sling and she got her act together.

Porters came from here there and everywhere, and so did officials who carried off the luggage, and so did soldiers who walked in front of them. When she asked why the soldiers were there, she heard that it was because the strike was far worse than before and nothing could be done except to wait and to see, and that was what you did in Brazil. They put her in a chair, and they went away. It was a good space, everyone had lots of space, but because it was first class everything was supposed to come to you. There were no shops where you might have gone to buy a drink. You had to buzz or phone or wait to get a menu or a list, nothing came to you and nothing could be taken out or in, you had to buzz, and then you might be ignored, a bit like a fly. The really terrifying thing was that it was almost empty, there were three men in the distant luxurious lines of seats, and no one else. But when she looked through the one way smoked glass wall she could see an absolute seething and suffering sea of humanity, they were moving like some obscene organic soup on the grounds below, random motion, plankton, waiting for a current, she thought. Then her left breast sent a horribly sharp spasm through her and she realised that this baby that had fed so well for a few days in England, had not fed properly for at least a month. Her breasts had grown from almost nothing over nine months to something which had made her feel, definitely womanly. Now they were like the plastic water bombs they had blown up as children, unreal explosives. The mobile rang:

'George.'

'Dominic.'

'What the hell's going on, I've been trying to get through for an hour. Look, I was wrongly informed, look things are badly off, there is no way out tonight, it's not a strike, it's something a bit more heavy.'

'What?'

'George, don't argue, just leave now.'

The phone went dead. George looked out towards the smoke screen, and the big black guard with a machine gun in front of it. She looked down at those skin tight breasts and started walking towards the guard. She got to the security gate, and a distant kindly voice told her to sit down and enjoy herself. When she said that her husband had told her on the mobile to leave immediately the voice said that all exits and entries were postponed, a strange word, she thought. The voice laughed gently and said to sit down, a terrible sign in Brazil. It was true that looking out over the crowd down below, through the smoked glass, everyone was going nowhere, running round and looking pretty desperate.

She sat down and turned back to the object in hand. She tried again to get Mathilda to latch on, but she seemed to be somewhere else, and definitely not wanting to drink milk. When George, in desperation, put a bottle of blood warm mineral water near Mathilda's mouth she drank some of it, although then she just threw it back, like a seal would throw a ball. George knew that this was not right, but there was no body to turn to, no one to help. She looked out both ways along the enormous vista of the corridor. It was a hundred yards, but there were three people; a large black man and his wife; a thin aesthetic man and his partner, a wizened old woman, probably his mother, and a young man in a jacket. George knew instinctively what to do. She moved to the thin aesthetic man, presumably an Indian, and his emaciated companion, and asked for help.

There wasn't much to be said on the face of it, simply that she had thought she was going to get the flight, that things had gone badly wrong, her husband could not get to her and she wanted to leave as soon as possible. They both smiled, and then the thin brown man told her that there was no chance of getting out of the airport that night or maybe any night in the near future. The new government had seen to it hat no one was going anywhere for a few days. He spoke with intelligent patience, but she could in no way concentrate, the baby was crying and both breasts were now beginning to ache quite determinedly, it must be the excitement she thought, but something's got to give.

Two hours later the scene was not noticeably different, with the exception that George had three times been to the women's toilets and three times failed to get Mathilda to open an eyelid. The air conditioning in the airport had gone completely, the lights almost completely, and the temperature was now creeping up into the early nineties, with humidity not far behind. She had tried phoning Dominic three times, the last time the battery on the mobile had died. Her supply of mineral water had gone long ago, and the drinking taps in the toilets no longer gave out anything. The Departures lounge was now entirely empty with the exception of the brown gentleman and his relative. The dignified old lady slept peacefully with her mouth opening and closing and opening and closing, on each breath, and a smile of unworldly satisfaction on her face.

George stared at her longingly, then down at the pained Mathilda, she looked at her for a long time and began to cry quietly, continuously, Mathilda was yellow and sweating. The pain in George's breasts was becoming unendurable, she could feel milk dropping out slowly from the nipples, but she could not suck them, and the occasional drop did nothing to relieve the agony. She moved her eyes from the child straight up, and they met those of the brown gentleman gazing at her with a not dissimilar expression from her own. Expressionessly she stood, carried the child over to the old lady, placed Mathilda beside her. She then unbuttoned her thin cotton blouse, eased one breast out of the cup, and sat beside the brown man. She squeezed the breast between finger and thumb and gazed at him imploringly. He gently moved his soft, bald, old, head down, he paused, removed his false teeth and placed them in her waiting hand. He stroked her breast gently with his hand and began to suck, with a relaxed neck and a greedy busy mouth, gently, purposefully. If you could have looked into their eyes at that moment you would have seen a sight. When they both understood that it was time to move on she covered the first breast, and gave him the second.

Two hours later the lights came on fully, and with much pomp, and dismissiveness, quite important looking soldiers arrived. Flights had been restored across the board, and order was again in place. Entering the almost deserted VIP lounge there were only two families in evidence. An elderly gentleman with his elderly relative, and a young mother with an infant in some distress. The young white woman shouted out her name and imperiously ordered a limousine to take her small daughter to the nearest hospital. She was, of course, immediately obeyed.

EGYPT

for Iman

Until today they had met only seven times in as many months, strictly a business relationship, at least for Mathilda. Mathilda worked in a shop called the Body Shop. She sold things to people which they then rubbed onto and sometimes into their bodies. She sold combs and things to comb through hair, she sold exfoliants and razors and shaving creams and all sorts of things to kill and cut hair. She sold real sponges and real loofahs, things of all shapes and sizes which had soaked in the briny deep, and things which now were rubbed across the English bodies, all shapes and sizes, which soaked in English baths. She sold cans which are sprayed onto bodies in the hope that these bodies will stay young looking or become nice smelling. It was one hell of a place to work, a shop about keeping your body the same and wanting to make it different, a kind of half way house. Mathilda felt that she was really the right man for the job, being half Scottish and half Egyptian. She was a drop down dead beauty, if you had a taste for the exotic, she was a strangely glossy, luminous, golden brown. You had to see it to believe it she was the colour, the texture, of a roasted pheasant fresh out of the oven without the grease on it. The most important part of her beauty came from inside, she exuded it, because she really loved her body, it continually fascinated and entranced her. She could not get enough of the smells she produced, the colours she contained, the way the bones moved under her skin, of her eyes like black diamonds or black gold, she loved her body, even its secretions, its blood, and each one of its dark black luxuriant hairs.

Working in the Body Shop was a godsend, she could experiment continually, free of charge, with all sorts of stuff, to take things away from the body or to add things on to it, or to disguise its various productions. Detergents, soaps, shampoos, deodorants, hair dies in powder or paste form, abrasives for sloughing off dead skin, or cosmetics for changing her colour, texture and smell. The options were seemingly endless. You name it and she had, at one time or another, had cause to try it. Her job was a delight with no beginning and no end. Her body became not so much a temple as a laboratory. Her experiments were frequently public, carried out in front of customers. She was so happy to demonstrate upon herself, and so serenely confident in the customer's desire to see her body demonstrated upon, that she was something of a star. Certain customers came in again and again. They bought certain things just in the hope that they would see that gold nail polish applied to the third toe of her sandled right foot. They would come to see a hand cream rubbed lovingly between the soft brown palms of her two embracing hands, moving in and out of each other like a nest of golden snakes. A certain young man came in with the most elaborate tale of a sick young sister exactly Mathilda's colour and age, for whom he had to buy a certain cologne which he would only recognise if Mathilda tried it on. They smiled at each other as he left because they both knew perfectly well that there was only one person trying it on right at that moment. Mathilda's smile was inimitable and infectious, it warmed the whole shop through. She had that inner light which grows out of having found contentment on a day to day, hour to hour, basis. Job satisfaction is a rare thing, and it brings its dangers. She was genuinely popular with almost everyone, but what some of the sales girls said behind her back, after she had got home, might not always have been music to her ears. But she wasn't thinking about that when she got home. She opened the door, ate, washed up, and then she continued her experiments in private. She lived alone, she was in fact a very private person when she was outside the shop. She had her own rituals for passing the time and what she got up to in the bath or before she went to bed, or when she was in bed, was nobody's business, so we won't go into that now, it's a digression, and anyway it's her own business.

To start again, as I said, Mathilda had met the woman only a few times. She had met her over the till, when she came into the shop to buy presents for her niece. She had asked Mathilda a few times for advice, and they exchanged a few words as the money changed hands. But today when she came into the shop she had her niece with her, a girl of about fifteen, and very pretty indeed. The niece, who was called Alice, had the relaxed flexibility, and glorious posture, of a young child, but definitely the body of a young woman. It was a figure that had grown, in all the right places and at all the right times. It was a body to note, to dote on, a body to prize. She wore a deftly cut nylon shirt, in a white and azure pattern that looked as if it had been lifted from a piece of Delft porcelain, in fact it had. The garment had tapered sleeves, and gently emphasised the open neck, drawing the eye down into the naked flesh which it revealed. She wore very tight hipster trousers made of a soft blue crêpe, with a wide elastic waist band which cut across her stomach, right at its very base, in a gentle curve. She could not have worn these trousers with any form of underwear, or the underwear would have been visible, which it visibly was not. She was a young woman who had thought a lot about showing off her body. Everything about her was inviting, she seemed to ask you to see through her, to look into her. She was transparently pale, a skin so fine that the veins were visible on her temples, and in the hollow of her throat. All these things Mathilda had noticed, with an almost painful and immediate precision, and she was still in the act of observing, when she looked up and caught the clear blue eyes of the other, older, woman, looking at her, or more truthfully staring into her. You only need that look once, and to return it, whether you want to or not, to know that you both know. The other woman showed unconcern, and turned her profile to Mathilda. She was the same colour as her niece, very compact yet slim, with a long straight nose, which her niece did not possess. She turned slowly and said brusquely:

'Come on Egypt, hurry up and choose and lets get out of here.'

Mathilda walked over to them and said:

'Can I help?'

The older woman repeated, in an amused tone:

'Can she help, Egypt?'

Egypt frowned, and explained:

'Well I want to get a face mask, do you have any of that thermal stuff, it's like magic clay and when you put it on your face it all heats up and brings all the blood to the surface, it's really tingly and hot, really weird feeling. It's great, all slimy and then goes crusty, makes you feel like a hippo having a mud bath.'

All three smiled, and the luminous Mathilda smiled again and said:

'We don't do that one here, because it's got some bad chemicals in it, and it's not Eco friendly. You'd have to go to one of those proper beauty salons, there's one further up the high street called Style is Everything, they'd have it.'

While she was saying this Mathilda was thinking how odd it was that this young woman was called Egypt. So she said, rather boldly, to the older woman:

'Is she really called Egypt, because I am half Egyptian?'

The older woman smiled, and looked that look again, and said:

'It's a family name, a pet name, because the first long word which Alice spoke when she was a baby was Lapis-lazuli, and the second was Tutankhamun. Ever since then she has loved Egyptian things, we still spend hours in the museum looking at the mummies.'

'Don't they frighten her.' Said Mathilda

'The big ones used to, but she didn't look at those, she didn't look at the grown up ones at all. She looked at the babies and animals, the child mummies, and the crocodiles and cats and ibises and jackals and fish.'

'Did they really make fish mummies?' Asked Mathilda.

'Of course they did, the Egyptians would make anything into a mummy, anything they believed in.'

Egypt burst in and said:

'Why don't we take her round and show her, are you doing anything tomorrow, Joyce will you take me again tomorrow afternoon. Anyway what's your name?'

'Mathilda.'

Egypt turned to Joyce and said:

'Can you take Mathilda too?'

Joyce turned to Mathilda and said:

'Would you like that?'

Mathilda said:

'Well I don't work on Sunday afternoon, and I would really love it.'

'It's a date then, the museum steps at two, or better still the bar of the Albion, opposite.'

Just as they were turning to go Joyce said quickly and quietly:

'I'll tell you in the museum another reason I call her Egypt.'

The museum was a great success, a real friendship seemed to be on the cards. Age and background were somehow irrelevant in front of those cool glass and hardwood cases, with their crisp linen linings. They stared wonderingly at the carefully laid out bandaged forms of dogs, cats, reptiles, fish and children. Bundles of dirty rags wrapping up the skin and bone of immortal gods, only a pane of glass between their eyes and all that mystery. It's a big thing after all, the mystery of a lost civilisation, and the full weight of it was inside Mathilda, because she had never actually seen a mummy before, let alone the mummy of a baby or a fish. It wasn't a time to speak, and everyone realised this, and so they drove Egypt back to her parents in silence.

When they were back in the car, inevitably, Joyce asked Mathilda round for supper. Mathilda went back with Joyce and in no time at all the wine was open, the music was on, the usual preliminaries. Suddenly both women felt unaccountably shy, the memory of that look in the shop had not left them, and returned like a ghost to freeze them into silence. They also realised that apart from the fact that they loved to look at each other there was very little to say. They were not curious about each other's past, or about what the other one thought, in fact the idea of finding out about each other was mutually terrifying. So Joyce said:

'I didn't tell you my secret reason for calling her Egypt, did I.'

'No.'

'Shall I?'

'Yes.'

'My father, not very long before he died, told me that Egypt was a code word which he and other soldiers wrote on their love letters home.'

'Why did he tell you that?'

'It was really unusual, it was a special occasion. He had taken me out to the opera, to Aida in fact. It was a treat, the night before I was going off to university for the first time. I was really nervous, and he was trying to make me feel grown up. You see after I came back from school, that summer, I had seen a lot of him for the first time in ages and we had become strangely close. He had never really wanted me to go to university, he wanted me to be a dancer. He said that you could use your brain at any time, but you could only dance once. He was a bit of a romantic in terms of what he wanted us to do, because he had had such a dull life himself, not to say he was a sexist old sod. So after the opera we went out to dinner, and he was smoking his pipe, and we were having a few drinks. And we started talking about the show which was pretty over the top, and stuff, and I said had he ever been to Egypt? And he said he hadn't but he loved the word, that it had a special place for him, that it was a word for him that was all about love and all about women. And when I asked him why he got embarrassed and he said, well he said it was a bit earthy. Then he laughed and said it was something he had always kept close to his chest. You see, Mathilda, it was a word he had put on letters to my mother for three years, and for him it was about missing somebody so much that you couldn't even think about it. And then he said it was difficult telling me now, because I was a beautiful young woman, but that he was going to tell me because he had always seen and felt that I was very beautiful, but he knew that he could never touch me, and that he would never touch me, not in that way, anyway. He had an astonishing expression just at that moment, the kind of expression you might wear when you are looking at something unspeakably disgusting, dead and rotten. Then he changed, in a flash, he really laughed, a kind of a hard barrack room laugh, and he barked it out…oh I can't say it…'

'But you must tell me now, what did it stand for, what did he say?'

'Oh God, I'm too embarrassed to tell you now.'

'All right you don't have to.'

Then Joyce said in a voice that would have moved mountains:

'Eager to Grab Your Pretty Tits.'

Mathilda snorted, this hit the spot all right and Mathilda and Joyce found themselves rolling on the carpet, while two brass sphinxes stared out from the fender with impeturbable, very riddlish, gazes. Laugher had come down like a bolt from the blue and possessed them, it shook them like a dog with a rat, it fed on them like disease feeds on a healthy body, it drained them and opened them up, it drowned awkwardness in something inhuman, it made them roar and howl, it made them shriek and grimace, it made them into something new, it threw them together and it threw them into each others arms. They had a laugh, they fell in love, they had a bit of the other.

A BRUISING ENCOUNTER

She weighed two hundred and forty five pounds in her socks, he weighed eighty five in his. She taught weight training in a gym, and could do more press ups than any of the men who trained there. He was training to be an airline pilot, and paying for it by free-lance photographic work for a big clothing agency. He was very good at commercial photography and very bad at flying. She was very good at lifting weights and very bad at listening. She came from Mona on the outskirts of Kingston Jamaica, in the foothills of the Blue Mountains. She had fought the early years of her life in a tin shed in one of the blackest spots on the face of the earth, or so she always said. She would expand the image, saying that Kingston was really more like a bursting sore, raging with hot disease, than a simple old spot. He had never been to Jamaica. He came from Royal Tunbridge Wells, one of the whitest spots on the face of God's earth, or so she said when he first took her to meet his parents. She said in fact that Tunbridge Wells was like a tight white blister, or a boil filled with cream white puss, sooner or later all that rot would have to come out like blood from a squashed tic. They both laughed at her crude attempts to rile him, and rightly so. Actually they liked each other, true it was a case of a tom tit on a round of beef, very black beef, but such things have happened since the world began. There's no accounting for taste when it comes to choosing our mates, and why should there be?

Anyway they were having a good time of it, both busy, both happy, both in love. What did it matter that day in, day out, they had to negotiate the same waves of disgust, hate and distrust, from just about everyone they came in contact with. The first time she had taken him out to meet her family in Brixton her younger brother had laughed in her face and said:

'Doreen, you crazy girl, no way can you fly with that Angel.'

Her younger sister, who was about half Doreen's weight, flirted outrageously with her new boyfriend. She called him onion, although his name was Jackie. She rounded things off by pinching him so hard on the bum, just before they left, that he had an egg shaped bruise on his left buttock which took a month to fade away. Doreen laughed every time she saw it and said it was a reminder of his brush with the dark continent. Doreen's mother and father refused to talk to her about the relationship, having made it plain that in their opinion she was playing a dangerous and foolish game. They saw her with some-one who could at best only be experimenting with her out of some misplaced sense of fun. They saw her with someone who, at best, was only half her weight. Then again they had a sneaking suspicion that Jackie must be some kind of a pervert, god knows what he was getting up to with their daughter, or why that little white freak would want to climb on such an outsized black girl in the first place. Jackie's parents were educated, and made a real fuss of Doreen, they treated her with meticulous warmth, and were unnecessarily open with her about the most intimate aspects of their lives, even their private lives. Doreen and Jackie would have long conversations about who was getting the worst deal out of the inlaws. Doreen finally summed it up by saying that while Jackie had taken it right up the jacksie she was getting the rough end of the pineapple. That made them both laugh out loud.

Things came to a head one day at seven in the morning. Doreen went out to bring in the milk and found a bucket of whitewash on the doorstep. When she tipped it away down the drain in a fury there was a large lump of coal in the bottom. The coal had a message sellotaped onto it, with sellotape bands going backwards and forwards right over the message to protect it from the white paint. It said:

'Nigger, love yourself.'

Someone, and she had a damn good suspicion who, wasn't being very nice. Jackie was really upset about how upset she was. He really couldn't understand what all the fuss was about, and he really could not see his own position as difficult. He loved someone, they were a different colour, so what, love has a right, love cancels out everything. Who gave a fuck about the racists out there, no matter what colour they were, blacks and whites hated each other, Doreen and Jackie loved each other, big deal. But Doreen was smitten, that message plagued her. She could not be sure where it came from, and she could not be sure what it meant. She was pretty damn sure it was her brother's nonsense. A white person wouldn't write something like that, unless they were saying 'Nigger love yourself', as in 'stick to your own kind' and then they would just write something like 'Fuck off Nigger'. But a young black person, who had been reading too much, thinking too much about the black man's burdens, would give you all that shit. She had heard her brother going on often enough about how it was black self hatred that was killing the black community, about how until blacks learned to love themselves for themselves, without even thinking about white people, and their crazy take on things, there was no hope. That little message slowly ate into Doreen, got under her skin. She didn't work out as compulsively, and she started to drink quite a lot in the evening and would then start up conversations, unnecessary conversations, about her life with Jackie. Things were starting to go badly wrong by the time we get to the crucial evening. The scene is as follows. Doreen enters the living room with three bottles of Beaujolais nouveau, she has already poured out two glasses, and is most particular, Jackie notices, to give him one, the left one. She then fixes him with a steady eye, raises her glass, shouts out 'lochheim', and they down their drinks in one. Doreen then sits down on the sofa and says:

'Onion, do you love me?'

She called him onion before her sister found out about it and high-jacked the word.

'Of course I do. He replied steadily.'

'I mean do you love my body, do you love my blackness?'

'If I love you, I love all of you, your colour and everything about you. I just love you.'

'But would you love me more or less if I was white.'

'More or less.'

'Don't fool around, I'm serious, and not more or less.'

'I don't know, surely I would love you less, because I love you exactly as you are and nothing that changed you could make you any better.'

'So underneath all the gallantry there is a clear point of view here, you only love me because I am black. Isn't that a bit kinky, given that you are white. Do you love yourself?'

'This is rubbish Doreen, this is logic chopping. I do love myself.'

'Do you love yourself as much as you love me?'

'Oh for Christ sake Doreen, this is stupid, you are just spoiling for a fight. These are terrible questions, they don't leave me anywhere to go. There is no right answer to anything you ask me. You are backing me into a corner, you get drunk in the evening and then you get this look in your eye, and away you go, always the same stuff accusing me of being weird for liking you because I am white and you are black, for Christ's sake, whose being the damn racist here? Can't you just live and let live like we used to?'

'Jackie, I just asked you a simple question, and all this bullshit won't throw me off the trail, I see through your smokescreen, you're still there and you're scared when I say, 'Do you love me more than you love yourself?'

'I don't know, who the fuck do you think you are, King Lear or something? What am I supposed to do, think again, speak again, nothing will come of nothing Doreen. You can't spend your time asking people to describe love, you just have to do it. Anyway this is so stupid loving yourself and loving someone else are not the same thing, they simply aren't comparable. How can a person ever know *if they love themselves*, surely someone else has to tell them, someone else has to stand outside and look in and tell them. But one thing's for sure, I don't think that you can love someone else unless you love yourself as well. If you hate yourself it's impossible to know how to love someone else, so if I love you I love me, and you're the person to know it Doreen, so you tell me, smart arse.'

'So, what do you want, you want me to stand here and tell you if you love yourself, talk about an egomaniac. You want me to stand there and sing a hymn of praise to the white ratty little fucking pilot photographer from Royal Tunbridge Wells. Look the question isn't about that it's about whether you love me because I am black, and whether you love yourself because you are white. And that makes it a pretty fucking serious question Jackie. Because which ever one you decide that you love the most, is going to be the victor. And the more I think about it the more I think you have to love yourself best because you are white, and that's what you understand. It's easy to pretend you're open to things, and that we are all, in principle free, when it's you who designed the fucking playpen, and invented all the toys. But black people don't always play in the same space, we try, but there are some hard cold dark historical facts that won't go away to do with people being raped on boats and thrown to sharks and shit, that just come floating back at us, and drown out the play pen, with no warning at all. That's not something you can ever look into, because it's ours. That suffering is ours, and not yours, you did it to us, and you can pretend to yourelves that you feel guilt about it, but at the end of the fucking day you are outside it, and you can't take it on. It's ours, it's our big dark playpen, and you feel as damn envious as you like about it, you can't get into it. There never has been and there never will be a great white jazz musician, and now you know why. And you know what I think, I think you only want to get close to me because you want to buy into that fantastic darkness, that massive misery, which is the precious inheritance of black folks, but remember curiosity killed the cat. Or maybe it's not even that complicated, maybe it's just plain vanity. I think you probably only tell yourself you love me because you are so damn self centred that you love the idea of exploring the idea that you love the opposite of yourself. And you just look at me like a laboratory rat. A big fat fucking black plague laboratory rat. And when the experiment's over, I'm kaput. You think that's a nice way to look at us, well do you?'

'Jesus Doreen, what's got into you. Have you been talking to your brother again, this sounds like exactly the kind of stuff he would go feeding into your head. This just is not you talking to me, it's someone else.'

'Look little Jackie, if I want to speak to my brother – don't interrupt me – I said IF I want to speak to my brother, about any subject under the sun, then I will and you are not going to censor my life, or tell me when I do or do not talk to my family.'

'OK so that's established, you did get this from your brother.'

Doreen at the top of her lungs screams:

'No, you smart little prick, this is not eff-fucking-stablished. I am not talking about anything except my right to talk to my family, any time, any place, any where, any way. If I've got to defend the right to talk to my family then the game's up. You took a few wrong turns tonight rocket man. I don't think I want to have anything more to do with you. I don't trust you anymore, and what you don't trust you can't love.'

While she is saying this Jackie starts singing the elephant parade song from the *Jungle Book* very loud. He's been feeling increasingly weird since Doreen gave him that drink, and he's sure that there was something pretty strong in there that wasn't related to French wine. He marches backwards and forwards singing out: 'With an up, two three four, with an up to three four, with a military air, with a military air.' He accompanies the chanting song with the most ingenious impression of an elephant you are ever likely to see. Doreen is enchanted, the anger falls away from her eyes, and all two hundred and forty five pounds of Doreen falls on top of Jackie and smothers him in kisses, and also just smothers him. A passionate night of love follows, Doreen is insatiable, and after about four hours, Jackie falls into an exhausted sleep, still sensible of the fact that Doreen is feeding on his body, covering every available area of his flesh with sharp bites and enormous suckings. Her fingers do not merely stroke but rake his body, or then knead him like dough. As he falls out of consciousness, lying on his stomach, Doreen is marching up and down his back doing the elephant impression, forcing the air out of his lungs with each plummeting footstep.

Jackie wakes up, he does not know how much later. He tries to look out but his eyes are bleary and so puffed up he cannot open them. He tries to sit up, but his stomach is agony, as if he has been bludgeoned in the guts. He can't even bend his knees or elbows easily. After about half an hour he manages to roll himself out of bed, and crawl to his hands and knees. He raises his eyes to the full length bedroom mirror and sees a small naked dark man, in great discomfort, kneeling in his place. The body looks more or less like his, but is swollen in places, the eyes like two puff pastries. The whole of his flesh has been worked over thoroughly, and not one inch of it but is covered in deep blue-black bruises. It is a fairly even effect, except around his face, where small pale patches, where the blood has died without discolouration, float against the dark background. Doreen has pinned a note to the mirror. It is the same note that was in the bucket of whitewash only Doreen has added an inscription. 'Onion, love yourself".

RUNNING A BATH, HER STORY

Like I used to go round there sometimes, like running around, like doing like shopping and things. I was about like ten and Foshun lived like alone. Foshun is like a funny name, and she said it in like a funny way, like tension, well like a man shouting in the army would say it, with his like arms like by his sides, like screaming, like 'TENSHON', or something. Foshun sat there in front of her old boiler, all fat and like shiny, like feeding it with coke all day, like coke, like who seriously uses coke any more, I mean like coal-coke, and what was coke, like really what was it like. This grey silver stuff in little bits of slippery grey, like someone had turded it out or something. I had to fill these huge old black buckets, like they were made of cast iron, like antiques or something, and I had to like haul them in, like they were seriously heavy, like weighing down on my arms, like stretching them out, like I was going to look like a baboon or something fresh out of the jungle, in no time at all. But Foshun she just sits there, in her chair at this like counter, and she swings these like big buckets up and over and across and down, like they were so many marshmallows, in one of those like plastic beakers, and she like slaps them down on the red tiles by her side, and then like tears into them with the shovel, like she was like digging her way out like escaping from Colditz, or after some like buried treasure, or like the crock of gold at the end of the rainbow, or something, and sometimes shaking like a whole bucket out like an avalanche, or like the Aberfan disaster or something, like shaking a whole bucket full of this like slack grey stuff, out onto the like roaring orange flames, sparks flying up the chimney, and then like smoke, like fuming up the chimney, like black thick smoke, like you would see in another time in another age like antique smoke or something like Sherlock Holmes, like a pea souper like drowning out the whole population of London, like a black grey green like slime, falling out of the skies and covering everything like until it was like ready to burst, or blow up, or something, and her big yellow arms shaking up and down, up and down, like a blancmange, or an egg custard, like inside this dress that she wore like tied all round her. When I say that she had like a dress, it was like a tent or a tarpaulin, or like something big, that had been outside a long time, like covering something up or something, it had this green grey greasy tinge all over it, like sheen, like a dead sea, all led grey. She had it tied up in about a thousand places, and the knots were big, like something wrapped up to protect it from the weather or something, like someone was really determined you were never easily going to get like inside it, certainly without like cutting the knots, but you would have had to be like really weird to want to get inside that thing, it wasn't clean. I started like thinking about what she was wearing underneath the big top, like there was room for a lot of wildlife in there, and as I like stood there watching those big bouncing arms, all like thick and like yellow, like paint on a road, and then I start thinking what would she like wear under the tarpaulin, like enormous frilly bloomers, like in an old fashion book, or like those tennis players used to wear, like Evon Goolagong, like so when they throw their arm up to like hit the ball you see this thing floating about like a lace jellyfish or something, and then I like think if Foshun wore something like that it would surely be a deal more like a giant like cauliflower, like sweating and smelling like of cheese, a bit like over grown, and going like yellow, like maybe even like a terrible orange, like the yolk of an egg, where it had got like really dirty or something.

When I start thinking this I start to feel like really sick at this moment, and it gets worse and worse, and like unbearable because Foshun lifts the bucket like back and she has all this like browny grey hair shooting like out from under her arms like a bush or something, or like one of those like big brushes made of twigs, on a broomstick, that they used to like smack kids on the bare bum with. And she has this like sheen sitting on her like most of the time, and her straggly hair, and this terrible like sweet smell, like rotten melons or something, like rotting smells come like floating off her, really like strong, and it's like always like hanging around the place anyway, and it hangs about me, like when I get out my friends like ask me like what crawled up my bum and like died, and I like don't reply, because I don't need to reply to that sort of stuff, but I still like think to myself that it's a high price to pay for a fiver a week, that's what I said, like a fiver a week, to come out like impregnated, like smelling like death, like literally like death itself, like I am like covered in animal corpse smell or something really horrible, like stale flower water, or rancid butter, like anything that has gone like seriously and like completely off colour. And I've got to think about like something, or I'll go like mad, and anyway I can like get my revenge on her by thinking about how on earth she like covers up her big lardy body again, and then the idea that she might like be wearing a thong like springs up in my mind, but it's not going to be anything like a thong, like a skimpy bikini type of thing, like they wear on sunny beaches, like in holiday brochures or something, no it's like going to be like a giant version of one of those like thick things that sumo wrestlers wear like up their bums, or like made of huge ropes, like ships' hawsers, or like an anchor cable, or something really massive, or if she was like wearing like normal elastic underwear, it would be like that horrible colour, yellow and pink, the cloth kind of fleshy beige, kind of colour, like the colour of the plastic they make false like legs and like teeth gums out of or something, and the elastic which was once white would have gone like yellow and like all spongy, like double yellow lines, like definitely no parking. And I really start to feel like a bit sick, like something is trying to climb out of my stomach or something, and so I speak to change the subject, and I say, like:

'Is there anything else you want Mrs. Foshun?'

And she says:

'No thank you not today.'

And I say, like:

'OK.'

Now one day I like come in and I am like standing there, like in front of Foshun, and she's like sitting by her fire, and its like gurgling away like in its usual way, like a drowning creature, and she like looks at me with this like horrible look, like looking through her eyes like in an 'I am going to stub my menthol cigarette out in your eye' look. Foshun smokes these like seriously unusual cigarettes, like San Morritz or something, that are like long and white with a thin gold ring and they come in this like beautiful packet, looks turquoise, or like the colour of a really like deep swimming pool in a brochure, and she smokes them she says for like forty years, and she smoked them because she says she like liked the menthol, which is like good for her health and like it makes her think of green running pools and summer and like horses in the trees and like stuff. Well I like know why she is looking at me like that, I should explain.

The reason for her looking the like electric chair look is like, well, this. Well Foshun has this like front room, and its all like curtained up, like drapes and pillows and cloth everywhere, and in like the middle is this table, like a little elephant, and its like piled with all these coins, like loose change, mountains of it, and in the middle is this one little pile of like shiny silver coins, and I just like slipped two of them in my pocket, and I know there is no way she can like see me, the door is like open a crack, a hairbreadth, and no one could see through it, not if they were like a normal human. So when I am standing there in front of Foshun, I like know I have like spent this money from last time, and so when Foshun says:

'I have lost two of my shiny coins, you wouldn't have a look on the floor for them, would you?'

I say, like:

'Of course Mrs. Foshun.'

And I like go through the big velvet curtain and like through to the front room, and I start grinning this like ratty smile, like a nasty sly ratty smile, and as I'm grovelling around on the dusty carpets, like scrabbling around under the sofas, and stuff, I am like grinning because I like know that there is no way I will find this money because I like spent it on a packet of Gauloises cigarettes for me and my like friends, because we were going to buy San Morritz, because I told them about banana fingers and her San Morritz and what they could make you like think about, and how they make you feel like totally on holiday, but then I just look at that like blue packet of French cigarettes, and it looks just like a summer sky, like the middle of July, like on holiday or something, and so we decide to like get the Gauloises, because they are like stronger anyway. And I keep on like scrabbling or ruffling around like I am going to build myself this like nest down in the corner or something, and Foshun shouts out:

'Come in here, come in here now this minute.'

And I come through and I say, like trying not to do the rodent grin:

'What is it Mrs Foshun?'

And then she like totally blows me away, like she gets her total revenge, and I cannot believe that I hear her say, like:

'Go upstairs and give the bath a once over would you?'

And I hear myself like thinking to myself, like 'Oh sweet Jesus', because I have never been like anywhere in this place except for Foshun's like front room and the boiler room, that's like what I call the room she lives in with the fire. And then I hear her like going on:

'And there's a sponge and some Ajax in the cupboard upstairs.'

And I hear myself saying, like:

'Yes Mrs Foshun.'

And then I hear her say:

'When you have finished run me a quick bath will you...'

And I think what a like ridiculous idea that is like a quick bath, and like Foshun and running, and like how can anything Foshun is like going to do be quick, or run, like unless its like scoffing down those little bins of marshmallows that she like wolfs down by the hundred, or those huge oranges she always like peels with her huge greasy fingers, with the sticky juice like running down all over her like fingers, like someone weeing themselves, or something, and those fingers, just like on the one hand, just like bananas, on one hand, I mean like one of her hands has like these fat fingers, that's why the kids call her banana fingers, when I like take her out for a walk. And like I can't bear the thought of the bath, but I've got to think of something, and so I like get back to the walk-ing, and think like about how I like take her out in this wheelchair, but it's not like any-thing you would ever see in a hospital, or like an old people's home, it's like a giant burnt out like pram or something, like some chariot that's been buried in the bottom of the sea, or like a bog, for like the last millenium, and I can't remember if she's got like big curved blades on the wheels, but it wouldn't surprise me because she like gets some serious grief from the locals, I mean like when you push it people like shout things out, like, pretty funny things, but I'm usually in like a spasm or something when I'm like wheeling her about, because she needs like a tank to pull her not me, because when you push it it's much bigger, or like heavier like a burnt out car, like a wreck with handles. Like she cannot do anything except haul herself on her big knubbly elbows like out of her seat and into this like chair cart, and I swear when her big like bum hits that seat, like it sends out clouds of smoke, or like dust or something like a building being demolished, and she like lets out this strange grunt, like the demolished building, like a tower or something, has like fallen on top of a bull and like squashed the life blood out of it, like winded it like for good. But she isn't in the wheel chair now, she is like right bang in front of me, and like looking a triumph look, like she knows what's in that bath and I do not, and its really a like straight game of dare, and I'm like not even on the starting grid.

And so I don't really have a choice like do I, because she's like outfoxed me, and like I can't seriously run out or that is like saying I am seriously like guilty, and anyway, if I am in like the doorway between the front room and the boiler room I can't go like anywhere, I can't like run out in front of her that is like saying I am guilty, and I just haven't got the bottle to go by her anyway, and I can't like go sneaking out of the front door like a criminal or something because it's got like this huge great curtain nailed down across it. And so I turn round and start up the stairs towards her manky old bathroom and I like get to the door knob, and like screw up my eyes tight shut like a kid watching a scary video, and like hold my breath, and like there it is. It's like this huge like caste iron thing, all like grey with like big feet like an elephant's, just like sitting there in the middle of the floor, and then I breathe like in through my nose and that like nearly like makes me sick, because this melon smell has got like seriously intense like you could like touch it like it's hanging like in the like air like all soft and like sort of like intimate, like horrible, like someone like stuck their finger like up their bum and like asked you like to smell it. It's getting really rank, I like can't breathe, like this must be like the melon smells like original breeding ground, or like mass grave, like this must be like it's home from home, like it's castle, and I peer over the edge into the bath and it's like totally disgusting, like all crusty, like an old meringue, or like tripes or innards or like something hanging down like all rubbery, and it's all yellows like old pee, or puss, or a leaking wound, a sick eye, God knows what, and I've like got to start thinking on my like feet or I am going to be like seriously ill, and so I start thinking that I don't want to have like the first thing to do with her bath or her ring, but that I must find the sponge, like first thing's first, and the like Ajax and that I take things like one thing at a time, like methodically step by step then I might just get like out of this alive. But then I like start to thinking like what is Ajax, like really, like I don't know, like it must be like something to clean with, but like what will it look like, like a paste, or a foam, or what not, like is it like a powder, or like one of those like really gritty things, but, knowing Foshun it's like really old, like antique, like Victorian or something, like the packet should be in a museum, like it will be all weird, like printed in blues and yellows, with a like thin woman in like a tartan skirt and like bright red lipstick, like blood red and sticky, and like massive like stiletto's and like a really like tight like white jumper, like it's part of her skin, and she's like holding this Ajax up which has like sizzly power lines like coming off it, like it's like seriously radioactive or something, and then I like start to like think about all the like people who have been in this bath before and like what they have like seen and done, and how this like bath has like a history that must like stretch way back beyond like Foshun and her like horrible lardy bum, and like how it has been like cleaned with this like Ajax stuff for like centuries, and then this like anger rises in me as I like think, like Sweet Jesus like how could Foshun like allow this like once pure like white like porcelain bath tub, this like antique, that should be like in a museum, to get so like filthy, so like seriously and like completely like loused up with like gunk, and like what was this like stuff like anyway, it just like wasn't like human, it was like God knows what, like was it even like from this like earth, like maybe she had it like brought in from another like galaxy or something and she was like an alien and it was like her like food, and then I like thought like this Ajax will have to be like really powerful, like dynamite or something, like you would need like a like really like strong like disinfectant combined with a like really like harsh like abrasive, like chunks of like volcano or something like floating in like dandruff shampoo to get this stuff off, and all sorts of like tools like wire wool, maybe like a paint scraper or like two, a like blow torch or like a flame thrower and like a crow bar at least, and then I like start to like think like it must like be a like sick joke like Foshun cannot like expect me to like get to grips with this stuff like she just could not like expect me like to do it, you would like need like a wonder fluid, or like a seriously smoking like acid, or like quick lime, or like Lysol, or like something some like serious like maniac would like throw like into a like bath to like dissolve like bodies or like something, and like then like my like mind like goes like like blank, like stark like blank like you like know like what I like am like thinking...

Horror, like real terror, just a blank a black and white blank. But like I must do something before I like start thinking about mass murders in normal houses, and like disasters, and fields of bodies thrown into ditches, and like people as soap bars and lampshades and bins full of gold teeth, and like the rest of it, but most of all I must forget two yellow feet, with horny toes sticking out of the end of the bath, while the stuff bubbles away, like it is being gently made into a stock or something. So I try and turn the tap on, to like take my mind off things, but Foshun must have been listening and has like sunk like to new depths, because I hear a voice like saying:

'Is everything all right, it's taking a long time?'

And I like say, like:

'I can't turn the tap on Mrs. Foshun.'

And she says: 'Why not?'

And I don't say anything, and that's partly because I like am really straining at this rusty old tap, but it like goes round as smoothly as clockwork until you get to this one point when it really sticks and makes this absolutely like horrible noise, like it's swallowing ground glass or something, and then I hear this terrible like grunting sound, and I am really quiet, and then I stop still and I hear this like terrible gasping and creaking and I can't believe it but she is coming on up the stairs, like breathing in this like terrible way, like she's making one of those like obscene phone calls or something, like when people phone you up out of the blue and say 'what colour are your knickers', it like happens all the time, and I can't believe it, I like freeze, and then like there she is, the closest thing to like standing that I have seen her, like standing in the doorway in this enormous pink dressing gown that is made of this like horrible shiny stuff, but she has got the big top still on under it thank God. And she looks at me and she seems to be like smiling, like this really sweet smile like a child, or something, and she says:

'All right, it *is* difficult, you can go home now.'

And I say: 'But don't you want me to give it a once over with the like... Ajax?'

And I don't know completely why I say this, it might be because I want to please her, or pretend to like please her, because I am shit scared and I believe she like might be going to really like kill me, but it's also because I am now like dying to know, like I really must like know what this Ajax is, like I would really die to know. But she like repeats, like in a really kind way:

'You can go home, I was wrong.'

And so I turn, to go down and out, but I look over my shoulder and I don't know if it's a trick of the light, or what, but there is one of Foshun's lower legs resting on the bath edge, that she's heaved up, like a tree, or a railway sleeper, and in this light I look at her face and foot, and they are died red, completely crimson, like the colour of a red red rose, and her foot looks red and shiny, like its been skinned or something, and the calf looks like a dead animal's body and the foot like a longish head, like a calve's head or something, and it looks at me and it smiles, that same sweet smile, through its white and red and bloody head.

And I turn down the stairs and go out, not a good day, not a good day at all. Well I only go one more time to see Foshun, the next week, because I feel that there is not really much more I can take, it's making too big a hole in my nerves.

And I say:

'Mrs. Foshun, I have come for my money.'
And she says:
'Yes, I think we both know what you mean.'
And I don't say anything.
And Foshun says:
'Go into the other room and wait for a minute.'
And I watch her through the door reach into this drawer with her big flippers, and take out this old fiver and this old bit of paper, and as she gives me the fiver I like cannot help grabbing the piece of paper at the same time, and I walk out, still wishing I had got to have a go with that Ajax.

When I am in the street I see the bit of paper is a photograph, a really old one. And there's this thin dapper black man, quite short, and this heavy woman, standing against a flat grey sea, with loads of big boats and cranes and winches and stuff in the background. And I look at the back of it, which has this printed name in bendy writing, Counter and Pelham, and then this inscription, Mr. William Foshun and Miss. Eve something, I couldn't read, the pencil faded out in to a single grey blur. And I looked back at the photo again, and Eve looked good, buxom, and motherly in her tight white dress, and staring out through her face was that same sweet smile like a baby.

DOCUMENTED

On January the twelfth of the year 2000 Jacob Panofsky walked into a private clinic in Rio de Janeiro, and on January the thirtieth Luisa Sardine walked out. After more than five years of painful and ground breaking surgery a new type of operation had been successfully performed. The treatment was carried out at the patient's demand, and was never repeated. Forty years later Luisa died suddenly of a massive brain haemorrhage, in a private mental institution in Lucerne, in which she had been living for fourteen years. For the previous twenty six years Luisa had been living a conventional family life, with a man who did not have any knowledge of her past. Despite the wealth inherited from her father Luisa never left her job as a medical administrator. Among her effects were three short manuscripts written on graph paper. The date of these writings is uncertain, and it has yet to be ascertained whether the composition of any or all of them can be established as occurring before Luisa's tragic fall out of reason. These documents have been donated to science by Georgina (George) and Dorothy Sardine, who have also agreed to leave their bodies to science. The daughters could throw no light on the chronology of the writings. Luisa's husband categorically refused to shed any light on any aspect of his relationship with Luisa before his recent suicide. They have been reproduced in the order in which they were discovered, sewn together.

I

Don't listen, just please don't listen. I want to get things straight, and I don't have much time or much of a choice any more, none of us do. I'm telling you this now, now that I think you are always within us. I need to talk, I have a special gift in that line, feminine intuition, patience, gentleness behind the eyes, a very nice smile that makes people who don't even know me, tell me everything. But that's not what I want today, today I want to talk to you, and get at some home truths. I don't want to be shitty, but sometimes I think that we've got some pretty big problems that need talking through, and you won't talk to me. In that sense you are like all the rest, the ones who won't listen and only want to succeed, and think that to do well you can't slow down and talk through all of your problems, show your feminine side. I have a good life and good things around me, and children, the most beautiful couple our friends say, and good births, I had perfect births. I did all the right things, in the right order, chanting mantras in labour, eating yoghurt, drinking raspberry leaf tea, doing yoga, aquarobics, aerobics, acrobatics, water planing and the rest of it, and I personally have thought my way through so many problems since my father died suddenly. I thought he loved me, but he didn't, he didn't know what it meant, to care for a child. He was work obsessed, living dangerously close to the edge, always playing up to the cameras, sounding good on very little, running in the fast lane on low quality fuel. Personally I don't care, I'm as safe as houses, I am rock solid, there is no way that there is anything they can do to me. I have earned respect from my husband and children, and shunned the eyes of the world. No one knows who I am, and I mean that, nobody. We live in a cosy place in a crazy world, and I'm strong enough to deal with it, I came through a school of hard knocks. There was no time when it wasn't a real world out there and I have seen enough, and I love it really, you look at all this stuff happening everywhere, bad things, violent things beyond anyone's control, beyond your wildest dreams. The earth kicking up a storm and millions die, or just sliding along in a train, in the middle of a civilised country for God's sake, and another train slides straight in, head on, and all hell breaks loose, hundreds incinerated in carriages no way out. Or sometimes it isn't even hands on, more like abstract disasters, money trouble just for the sake of argument, financial disasters so huge you don't even think about your personal savings. Or if you do it's all about how safe you know they are, safe as houses, and that's so selfish. But is it, is it really, isn't stability our savings, isn't it the fact we do buy cars the thing that keeps most people in the world at work? Someone told me that that was the case, quite recently, they were drunk, at a party, or not quite themselves, and I can't give up my car, and what next anyway, there are bigger troubles, many worse things happening, out there. There is trouble in the desert, trouble on the mountains, people squashed in the snow, people falling out of the air and the rest of it. Whole cities burning and falling, and in those situations everything goes to the dogs. I have seen the pictures, heard the words, or voices beyond words, humans making the sounds of animals, so sad they can't even speak a word any more. Children suffering and dying in droves, all colours and all shapes and sizes, lying at the road side, big eyes too dry for tears, no one and nothing can help, but it's not for me to say. All I'm saying is that in a world like that why not take a few chances, walk the line. I'm not going silly, but I have a point about how dangerous things are getting. Someone told me that you are safer in an aeroplane than any other space on the planet now. The thing to work your way into is the perpetual business jet, nothing could get you, and in it nothing could get you so fast and so safely, out of danger. Nowhere and no time, just sit back and watch it all happen, enjoy the ride, that's what they said with their arm around me and my arm around them. It's not black and white any more, it is a minefield out there. It is not just a question of looking out for number one, we have much bigger fish to fry, a bigger responsibility, and a bigger opportunity, bigger. You work, you play, you work for a living, without it there is no living, work or play, while you live that's what we do, unless you are mad or very very rich, and stupid. Then there's no new way of living, you have to basically come up with the goods, bring home the bacon, and do yourself a favour. It is true, we are all powerless, in the face of many forces we do not understand. The most important is dying, and it is true we live with the body machine factor, but so what, what are we a factory, a tractor? No we do the best we can, in a world that could be sweet, if only, if only the right things happened to all of us for all of us. What went wrong, what is the problem, who is right and wrong, who is weak and who is strong, who is gay and who is straight? We don't care, quite rightly we don't care, we do our best and I hope to be doing the best I can. Under the circumstances, and what circumstances, what can anyone expect from anyone, not a lot, we know, but with the right levels of trust so much could happen. I get the feeling that we all totally love each other really, deep down inside, where the blood is thicker than water, but the language is just slipping away, beyond us, beyond me. I will have to find a new way of talking. I know we all talk a foreign language really. That was a nice thing a friend said to me quite recently, they weren't quite themselves, and I vowed not to forget it. They said: 'who can communicate with who, does anything understand anything else, and why would they want to anyway?' Good questions, I thought, and no one has the answers. I know that there are problems, big, big problems, but why are we sad, all the time. There really is no need. I'm not sad, I've had my ups and downs, but I have a clean bill of health now, a clean pedigree. I love to work, that's what gives me my freedom, why shouldn't I, I've worked hard enough to earn the right to work.

II

Maybe if I calmed down a bit things would be different, maybe, if I took a deep breath I could see things in a different light, I should take things a day at a time, step by step, one foot before the other, drop by drop, no running before I could walk, or I'll end up with one foot in the grave, maybe if I just cooled down a bit, I would be all right, every cloud would have a silver lining, I could start with the simple things, like sharpening my own pencil, but a little bird tells me that they won't even let me do that again, not even sharpening my own pencil, my card is clean, I don't worry about my pedigree, if I' m talking to myself then it's the first time I ever did and it's the best thing I've ever done, there comes a point, there comes a point, where you really have to talk about it, stand up for yourself to your-self, maybe I just worry too much about what they think about me, but that's a woman's disease, straight out, what do I care, but then I always have this sneaking suspicion that they only look at me that way because I have a hole inside me, because I can have chil-dren, because I have had children, the biter bit, the breeder bred, and why shouldn't I, why make a big deal out of it, half the world does it, and it doesn't amount to a hill of beans, why separate us out over a thing like that, jealous, the only men in this place can't have children, and the only women in this place won't have children, so where does that leave me, a freak, all dressed up and nowhere to go, or maybe it's gone beyond that, maybe they all think I'm going through the change, changing from a breeder to an old lardy disaster, a flood of hormones going down the chute, and another lot coming in, breasts withering, moustache sprouting, hot flushes, big mood swings, and no more power to generate, well what's all the noise about, it's not such a big thing, the differences are greatly exagger-ated, but it might be something entirely different, just a nasty desire to wear me down, see if I can still hack it, sometimes you know I don't think they even think about sex, it's not part of their make up, androgenous androids, pure neuter, day in day out, it's a dog's life, you'd have to be a neuter to do it, I kidded myself but it always was, always will be, and worse than that, because you wouldn't treat a dog like that, just chucking stuff at them, pile after pile, you wouldn't treat a rat like that or even a fish, a fish in a tank, or anything, not the lowest thing you can think of, worm, caterpillar, boll weevil, a slug, a piece of jelly that was barely alive, the worst kind of a child molester, a pervert, a pariah, a dirty dog covered in tar and feathers, even a woman, you would show some respect, sometimes let it go its way, let it put its horns out, wag its tail, let it have a bit of rope, let it crawl off into a corner and lick itself into shape, that's the way, always putting me on the defensive, putting the wind up me, putting me down, if only they would put me down, like some toothless old bitch, I wouldn't be the loser, no way, they'd finally see what they'd lost, too late to pick up the pieces, they lost a gold mine when they lost me, they'd have to make the best of it then, no I'm not the animal they think I am, they are the animals, feeding feeding away in dark corners, greedy, sub-human, gremlins, robbers, bloody day-light robbers, spooks, goblins, or not even that dignified, not that grand or frightening, no not frightening, bloody terrifying, vampyres, blood suckers, dirty mixers, dogs in the manger, mingling blood and poisoning the whole bloody planet, after it all the time, any-thing with two legs or four, or just pretending, silent like whispering death, no, no a lot more like some disease, like a big greedy tumour the size of a walnut, or a tomato, or a melon, or a potato even, like something soft and rotten, that's got no right to be alive, but there it is feeding off the fat of the land, lodged there, at the top of the tree, straight up to the top of the greasy pole like a ferret up a drainpipe, climbing to the top of my head, slowly, unstoppably, living the high life, always at someone else's expense, while they're having such a nice time living the life of Reilly, who picks up the tab, who does the real work, who does the dirty work, who picks up the dirty laundry, who is grubbing in the back room sweating over a hot stove, who gets stuck holding the baby, who gets thrown out with the bath water, whose got to pay the price for all this fun and games, all this high kicking and all this fancy footwork, dead end, no way out, it's not even worth asking the question, because we all know that it's always been like that, winners and losers, people making the trousers and people wearing them, bloody savages wearing trousers, bloody cannibals, blood suckers, but they don't fool me, well you can only hit your head against a brick wall so many times, you can only go on banging away for a while, everyone only has a certain number of head bangs in them before something gives out, there's a short and a bulb blows, the fairy on top of the Christmas tree gets blown to kingdom come, there's a short-fall, or a fucking long one, the system fails, the family falls apart, there's a major decline in standards, and the brain just stops giving of its best, it fades, it withers, burnt out like an old battery, its virtue disappears in a cloud of mist and rot, a stinking chemical miasma, a plague wind of loss and blind hopelessness, nothing to do and no way of doing it, not in their language not according to their rules, and your head goes down, you can't keep your chin up, you're sailing into a head wind, you can't keep your pecker up, no way, and then you're no good for anything anymore, quite simply knackered, shop soiled and damaged goods, no one wants that stuff anymore, not at that price, no one wants to smell that anymore, no not anymore than they want to suck on an old fish dinner, put their head in a bin liner after a party, fuck a corpse, but that's the way they want it to go, that's the trap, that's what they do, that's what they've always done, why change now when they have always known how to keep the cards close to their chests, when they've always held the trumps, when they make the plays, and invent the games, all the fun of the fair, but they know how to wear you down, but do they know why they do it, that's the only hope, that's the needle in the haystack that you've got to cling on to for dear life, that's your bird in the hand, keep kicking against the pricks, chancing your arm, it's not going to do any good, but you do it anyway, resist, resist, when all around have lost their head, you can't turn the tide back, the mountain doesn't come to Mohammed, they are intractable, unstoppable, they don't need to answer any questions but that does not stop them from, nagging, going on, keeping on, keeping it up, keeping their horrid end up, right up in the air, having a go and always trying to get me to show my hand, or even, to put it more crudely, my end, and the lengths they'll go to are nobody's business, double crossings, and bluffs, and double bluffs and triple bluffs, ruses you wouldn't believe, moving the goal posts and taking the net down, digging up the pitch, and all sorts, up to their tricks, slippery customers all right, slimy bloody slippery devils, getting me to do what I don't know how to do, worming away, no stopping them, questions, questions, never with the decency to ask me straight out, always paper and letters, a stamp for this and a stamp for that, and this smile, this decent smile, and all the time, it's as plain as daylight, as plain as the nose on your face, that they're trying to get inside my pants, or maybe not even that, just to frighten the pants off me, to scare me to death, put the fear of almighty God into me, or maybe its not so simple, maybe it's all a test of nerve, a trial by combat, a trial of strength, the eternal battle of the sexes, winners and losers, *unum inter pares*, to see if I've got the bottle, the nouse, the sheer bloody three o'clock in the morning courage, they want to back me off into a corner and see if I'll stand up and be counted, start punching blind, see what it really looks like when the worm has turned, when it goes savage and shows its true colours, bares its teeth, goes completely tropo and takes a good hefty bite out of one of them, takes their ear off with a snap, that's the test, and I should take that test, I should take a stand, have a go, stand up to them, take a swing at them, get my gloves off, and give it a go, make them back off, for once and all, make them kick and then I'd show them how I kick back, a stiletto heel to the temple, Emma Peel style, that would wake the bastards up, the trouble is that they have the advantage, looking down from the high ground, from their ivory tower, so that I don't know if I'm coming or going, every which way but loose, they haven't got the right, going at me and never a break, if I had the time to stand back, to think it all through I tell you it would be a very different story, I'd outfox them at the final hole, the tables would be turned, a new set of values, I'd have them at it, no let up, the chickens would come home to roost and the meek inherit the lot, the whole sodding lot, the little children, justice with vengeance, blood lust and the rebel yell, the red mist comes straight down like a sheet anchor, sheer bloody mayhem tumbling down the rocks, apocalypse, millennium, sulphur pools, torture, the silk scarf and the rupee, as mad as a meat axe, straight into them, a totally loose cannon, spinning round like a catherine wheel, literally ankle deep in blood and firing off a few salvoes point blank, some big shot right in their faces, if it goes on this way it will come to that, a mother's instinct, and don't say you can tell me that you haven't been warned, although I'm loathe to let the cat out of the bag just now, there was a time when, but why tell, why should I tell any of this to anyone, patience, that's how you'll get them my beauty, catch them napping with their pants down, and nowhere to go but down down down, yes, oh yes, let them think about it, let them think about this one, when you're at the bottom the only way is up, but it takes so much energy just to keep still, just to swim against the tide, just to tread water and keep an even keel, just to touch bottom, I just don't know what to do, maybe take a rain check, spend a day at home, cooking something or doing some baking or that sort of thing, throw them a real curve ball and go back into my kitchen, make a cake, don't ask me what sort, any sort, a big heavy thing, like a huge rich turd of a cake, like a Christmas cake, as rich as Croesus and as heavy as a lump of clay, get a few friends round, have a party. Sitting here you lose all sense of perspective, all sense of the landscape outside, I really wonder where I am at times, sometimes I forget where I am and what it's like outside, if there is an outside and an inside, is the sun shining, is it day or night, am I on the shore, or in the sea, is this an experiment or is it real life, doing a job getting paid, keeping the wolf from the door, does that make sense or doesn't it, if they expect me to do all this for nothing and look after the kids then they've got another thing coming and the fat will be in the fire, the shit will surely hit the fan, sooner or later I will get to the end of the tether, I'll stop towing the line, I will slip it, I will lose it, I'll swing the lead out full fathom five, stop the rot and stop putting my paws in the air, stand up on my two hind legs, bark out something pretty damn sharp, give them the eye, break out, confront them, make them face up to me, face up to the ugly facts, get them into a barny, needle them, play on their weaknesses, tweak the Achilles heel and twist the knife, they'll give the game away, go belly up, even then will they realise that I'm not just a pretty face, a nice pair of tits, that I have feelings too, that I am a fully fledged human being, only one thing holds me back right now and that's that if you have it all out in the open, if you bare your all, then you're the vulnerable one, you're the one whose showing off your wares for all to see, *force majeur* has its dangers, its drawbacks, and it could go either way, maybe I'd be floored, maybe they'd pull out something special, maybe they'd pull the rug out from under me, whip it right out from under my feet and I'd be arse over tit, and maybe I wouldn't even know what hit me, they'd blow me out of the water, break a walnut with a sledgehammer, a butterfly on a wheel, and that would be that, not even a ripple, not even a drop in the ocean, not a pretty sight, or worse, maybe they wouldn't even see, or pretend they couldn't see then start laughing gently, men and women, girls and boys, lords and ladies and gentlemen, the whole shop floor, the whole shooting gallery, maybe they couldn't even be bothered to laugh, just squash me like a toad, swat me like a fly, stick me like a pig, stuff me like a turkey, put my head on a platter with an apple in my gob, shoot me down like an albatross, you couldn't do that to a person without feelings, but you can't be sure they have feelings and if they don't then it's not a game you can play, you're not even in the same ball park, you're not even on the same planet, there is no common ground, no way out and no way back and they can't have feelings, you just could not behave that way if you have feelings, real human feelings like love and hate and warmth and love and tenderness and joy, sorrow, sadness, melancholy, or even basic instincts, hunger and fear desire, lust, yes lets forget their filthy propriety, let's talk a bit dirty, let's hang out the dirty linen on the line, hang up a few naked skeletons in the wardrobes, see what smell comes out of the blot on the Scutcheon, to tell it like it is let's quite simply bring a bit of sex into this, if they're always trying to look up my skirt, get inside my pants, feel my legs, let's turn the tables for once, let's get dirty, punch below the belt, what do they think I am, some sort of a female castrate, a fucking castrato singing blind for my supper, not man or woman, some sexless thing like a slug or a sea cucumber, something that fucks itself, what a thought, what a thunderbolt to come out of the blue and pass through my mind, but has anyone ever looked at me and thought that this person, this figure, in the brown suit and the magenta knickers, is a sexual being, a fully fledged sexual person, have they ever thought that that's a nice piece of meat, a bit of all right, fanceable, tasty, a bit phaaw, something that knows what it wants and knows how to get it, a natural born woman, have they ever looked at me and thought what I look like under that brown suit, pretty damn trim, pretty nice buns I can tell you, well that's not the way forward but I know a thing or two about the opposite sex, any colour, any place, any time, I'm not choosy, the sap's always rising in this spring chicken, I can tell you, you fucking doubting Thomases, but like I say that is not the way forward, that way madness lies, I can tell you, start thinking like that and sooner or later you miss the A train, you get left behind, flotsam and jestsum, the tasks build up and the molehill becomes a mountain, and you can't even begin, it all gets too much and you're on the scrap heap before the day even starts, a letter or something like that, they send you a letter, and it says, the end, kaput, finito Benito, we don't want you we don't need you anymore, you don't belong here, with your long eyelashes, and your painted nails and your damn droopy look, and your softness, and your periods, and your mood swings, and your basic instabilities, you don't belong anywhere, you're not even good enough to be rubbish, you're no good, at your job, or you're just a misfit and you've misfired, backfired, just plain fired, and so we'll look straight through you, like you don't exist, not even unpleasant just blank, a black hole, a white noise, well it's not that bad yet, but maybe that's the weak link in the chain, maybe that's all arse about, you can't know what's bad and good, what's that bad and that good, you can't put it down in words of one syllable, you can't put it down at all, the thing to do is not worry about bad, but think about the worst, rock bottom, when the plug is pulled out, when you are up the shit creek up to your throat cut out in the shit, there is still no point thinking that it's bad and going to get worse just think that this is as bad as it gets and multiply by ten, so what, so damn what, that's the way, I'm ready, I'm game for that, I'm game for a laugh, that's when you start singing, that's when the glory days begin and you come up stinking but clothed in the sun, yes what if it was, yes really what the fuck if it was, would it really break my heart, would it tear me apart, would it break me up, would I be gutted, is that all there is to be frightened of, well if that's all it is, if that's their best shot at the end of the day, they can take a hike, take a flying fuck at a rolling doughnut, they can realise that when the chips are down the steaks are small, and would it all be crystal clear, would they see that they're rumbled, barking right up the wrong tree and barking mad, that I see that the only thing that seems to make them tick is the fear that they won't bring home the bacon, well what if you don't bring home the bacon, what if you come home empty handed, what if you look in the cupboard and it's bare, the worst that can happen is you starve to death, and so what, is that a fate worse than death? Well that's it, I'm not a blind mole, a bat, I'm alive and kicking and up to the job, you can't do that to me for a lifetime and it not take its toll, you'll pay the ultimate price, I've got what it takes to really take the bull by the horns, do it my way, I can fight my way out of a corner, duck and weave, throw a few faints, play dead and keep my weather eye open.

III

Well that's how things stood. Backwards and forwards, hither and thither, no way out and no way in, no way up or down, sinking or swimming it was all the same, going round in circles, going nowhere fast, sucked into the vortex. They weren't winning but I surely as there is a sun in heaven, wasn't losing either. Things stood in the balance, and something had to give. I needed a break, a shot of something special, a kick up the backside to make me see my way out. I looked out of the window, and it was the twighlight hour, neither night or day, hot or cold, and there was this heavy grey cloud cover, and I looked down at my pencil, and it was sharpened, a lovely cone of grey. Then I saw them come up to me, pushing this thing at me, and wrinkling up their nose, like a big black rabbit. That's when I slammed that pencil into their eye, with all the strength I could muster. That's the way the cookie crumbles, and that's how things stood, backwards and forwards, no way out and now no way in, floating sinking or swimming it was all the same to me, I looked out of the window, and it was neither night or day, pefectly grey. I looked down at my pencil, and it was sharpened, to this beautiful, point sharpened in this electric sharpener. A lovely machine had made this perfect cone of grey. That's when I saw them come up to me, pushing right up close, in my face, breathing on my face, pushing this thing at me, and puckering up their nose, trying to look friendly like a fat white rabbit. I rammed that pencil into their eye, with all the strength I could muster. I can see clearly now why I did it, why I did it all.

CASTES

'I had a dream, I was thinking about why we once thought we knew we were really suited to each other, I mean beyond sex, why we went further and thought that we fitted each other, hand in glove. I went to sleep, I fell asleep, in the same bed as you, yet feeling a sad basic dislike of you, as usual now, as mutual now. In fact, as usual these days, turning my back on you, and moving as far as I could towards the edge of this very uncomfortable bed, in this terrible heat, I began to fall asleep, and then I had this dream.'

'Do I need to know about it?'

'Well I can't remember it exactly, so that's a difficult question to answer. I know I was thinking in the dream about why we were together, why we lived together and what this meant. Why do we do it, why did we ever do it, did we believe in love or something? Did we come together and then grow apart, or were we always apart, knowing we must die alone, no matter what, we must die alone, and that we would fool ourselves into believing in permanence, in partnership, in some kind of trust, or fear, I don't have a clue, what was it, I just don't have an inkling?'

She contorts her mouth into a hideous shape, like a parody of a guffaw, and makes the sounds of human sadness – crying – sobbing – howling – weeping – bawling – snivelling – just crying really. He sits up, and like a cartoon character, actually rubs his eyes, and says:

'Is this the dream or you dreaming about the dream, or you trying to deeply piss me off? Why can't you just tell me about the dream?'

She continues:

'Give me a break. Wasn't this the point of our whole, so called, holiday. I was trying to talk about a dream about my anxiety about us. It was a dream about origins, about why we did what we did. Since everything went pear shaped, or we lost control, or we started to see the truth, or whatever it was that went off, badly off, I think I have changed, and I think, I really sense that I can think about new things. I mean why do people insist, ever, in the first place, on actually living together? That's kind of a big question, why do they do that and then pretending that they have the same tastes, and keep on trying to make themselves like the other person that they don't even really know, because you just can't, your body can't, or on trying to make the other person, the other, like themselves. Its just a joke surely, just some sort of an aberration, all just a trick of the mind, which some power puts over on us to convince us to have babies, just fucking away, like animals, as couples, in couples. Or, look don't get me wrong, maybe I got the whole thing wrong, the baby thing isn't actually that important. Maybe it's a bit overrated by everyone, or just an excuse, like a relative dying, or a natural disaster or whatever attracts your attention as something out of the ordinary. I mean, I know that we never were able to have one, but basically that's not the point of why people inevitably start it all up in the first place. I mean, being together, and then not.'

She looks sad, and the story of the dream appears to be no nearer to him. What makes him speak is that he can't bear the weight of those eyes, so he says:

'It's early in the morning and we didn't come here, on that terrible flight, it's a long way, just to go through the same old stuff. You can't take it anywhere, I mean you can't take it everywhere. We came out here to give each other a chance, to try to get some kind of perspective on things. Yes we did really want to have a baby, most people, in their heart of hearts, if they are young, and have enough money, like us, really do. Yes we did try every trick and turn which modern science could provide us with. No there is no earthly reason why we couldn't have children... I never worked that out, the earthly reason.'

He stops, while she scratches herself, then he continues, talking loudly, not to anyone in particular, not even to himself, he's in mid flow:

'If it's not an earthly reason then is it an unearthly one? Shit that really irritated me so much, even a top fucking consultant, paid Christ knows what a minute, and he sits us down like kids in some kind of an obscene birds and the bees initiation talk, in the middle of his ridiculous antique laden private consulting conversation room, and he then says, in his weasel voice, which I cannot forget: "You do realise, Dominic and Deborah, that there is no earthly reason why you cannot produce a child, Deborah can conceive, and, Dominic, you have an average sperm count." And I cannot forget that stupid sentence. What is the, this, that earthly reason, if there is no earthly reason why we can't have children, then what the fuck have we been up to for three years? God only knows, God and his-fucking-majestic-self on his earth, and its earthly fucking reason only perhaps know, what we were up to.'

He has ended the speech standing close to the blinds, and holding out his hands, waiting for something, he goes on:

'After all this, why did you get me started? Why bother? I don't know why we can't have a child, the question is, the question is, *is that* why our relationship blew up in our faces the last two years? Look, I don't want to talk about this now, OK, the dream is fine, the dream is OK I will always be interested in your dreams. But you haven't told me it yet. Please just tell me the dream.'

After a moment she begins again:

'I'm sorry, I wasn't trying to get you started, I know that's a bad beginning, but I wasn't. I had this really terrible dream, OK, and I was trying to work it out. It was definitely about children and relationships, but I think I was being told something important in this dream. Look I know this is totally naive, and that dreams can't tell you something everyday, or just simple, without a whole load of stuff coming in to tell you what a dream really is outside just silliness. But listen. Someone or something was just warning me off some basically misinformed stuff. Basically asking about the partnership obsession, this dream, I don't think it's about sex, or the fear of loneliness, or any of the old excuses, I think it's about the fear of experimenting. I think it's about the Western obsession with cutting down, cutting out your options. So I am not attacking you, but what you just said convinces me that our problem is that we're too fixated on the idea of the love for life thing.

'You mean our fucking relationship.'

'I suppose so. Just, the assumptions, like bonding, single couples, coupling again and again, with the same person, to produce some kind of breed, that you call a family, isn't that just a little bit unnatural, why is that what you want? I mean what if everybody felt that it was normal to have at least one child with four different partners, and that each of these partners, for the future health of the planet, had to come from an entirely different race, would that be a bad path to take? And I mean men and women, they both have to shop around, do their best to the best of their ability.'

There's a silence; he doesn't know if it's early in the morning and she is just trying to wind him up, or if it's early in the morning and she is just being hung over and daffy. She doesn't know either. She doesn't know if she is saying what she thinks, or if what she is saying is what will make him sad and angry, and that is what she thinks, and that she has to say anything to make him sad and angry, because that will get him talking. And he hasn't been really talking since they got on the plane and they both realised that for three weeks they had agreed there would be no escape. So they spend the first day walking around near the airport, and talking and thinking about how hot the air and the sun is on their skin. They go to bed, they sleep on opposite sides of the bed. If anyone could look down on their bodies as they slept they would see two forms, labouring sadly to fall asleep, most of the time they think about sleep, while being horribly aware of the waking form of the other, a heavy human body tossing and sweating, only inches away. A once loved and familiar form, now an object unbelievably far away and colossaly repugnant.

As soon as he is sure that they will both admit to being awake, and as a milky green light enters the room, he says, too loudly.

'I hope that you remember what I'm talking about, I've been thinking about it all night, what I'm saying, is about what you said yesterday about shopping around. It begs a few questions, like are there different races anyway, a lot of people don't believe that any more, and how would you enforce this on people who didn't want to mix and match, even for the cosmic health of the planet. There are a lot of women now who don't want to have one baby, let alone four.'

She looks up wearily with those terrible eyes and says:

'Look I wasn't talking about implementing a regime here, I was speculating, and thinking not how do I make this happen, but what if it did happen, what if it was the norm, simply what every human being was born to do. In a matter of a few decades what would the world be like. If you could really have a go and everyone have a go with everyone else...'

He cuts her short and replies:

'Over populated, in a word.'

'No, I don't think so, I mean think of all the Indians and stuff who are having at least eight or ten kids at the moment, if they only had four that would leave a lot of room for everyone else.'

'So was that your dream, your really badly racist dream about the Indian sub-continent, cut down on the darkies breeding so we can produce more light skinned European half breeds, or are we talking about something else now?'

There is a silence, it's been a long time a coming but now she'll tell him, in so many words, about her dream:

'I'm trying to remember my dream. It was Christmas, snow was falling outside a large window, like a shop window, and a group of men were outside, and a group of women were inside, and the women were all naked, like one of those shop windows in Amsterdam. And the men were gazing at the women and the women were looking at nothing in particular. Now every time a man saw a woman who he thought he really wanted, he started to change colour, like a really bright plasticky sort of colour, day-glow blue, fluorescent yellow, traffic light red and so on. The woman who was being thought about didn't change colour but her eyes began to glow, but not always the same colour as the man's. And this small baby, the same colour as the man, would slowly bulge out of the top of his head, like a tumour or something, and float up into the sky. Up in the sky was a big flat disc, like a discus, smooth and shiny, and on the disc were millions of these little fantasy babies which could have been made out of the man's desire but never now would be. Each baby had a placard, with neon lettering telling the story of what it might have been, had it come into being. Then all of a sudden the sky opened and a rain of sort of deep yellow brown paint or clay or something came down and deluged everything, blanked everything out in the colour of shit, even the shop windows, and that was the end of the dream.'

There's a silence and then he says:

'Well don't ask me to read it, we didn't come all the way to Mexico to lie in bed half the day and un-pick your dreams.'

'Why did we come all the way to Mexico.'

She says, and he replies:

'The simple answer is to try and fool ourselves into believing that there was something left in our relationship. Or at least think about what was still left alive that we could try and work on, without killing it in yet another bout of mutual recrimination. The real answer is, that at the very least we might get some sun and some culture. Talking of which what do you fancy today, more colossal heads, of which to tell you the truth I am heartily bored, or the Quinta Olvidados. And here I quote, "The Villa with its unparalleled collection of colonial and folk paintings. The collection has many highlights. It includes all the extant works produced in obscurity by count Alba, when the villa was a mental sanatorium for aristocrats. There is also a complete set of the renowned Castas paintings, celebrating the union of races in eighteenth century Mexico. This cycle, known locally as *Os Pumos*, is widely regarded as the finest in existence." Actually that sounds right up your street, a bunch of paintings about interbreeding in Mexico made a long time before you were a twinkle in your mum's engagement ring.'

She speaks with eagerness for the first time:

'Castas paintings. What are they, have you seen any?'

'Never heard of them, all it says here is what you just heard.'

'Oh I just remembered the other part of my dream.'

'Look, later, if you want to see these pictures we've got to rock and roll or the sun's really going to get a head start on us, and everything will be closed.'

In the long dining hall of the white stucco mansion their eyes slowly become accustomed to the dimness. Along the wall stretched rows of paintings, paintings from Mexico before the words gringo or gringa existed. Generalissimos in stances of wooden rectitude, Majas with small dogs and black boys, angels holding impossibly tapering flintlock rifles, titanic bowls of fruit looming out against ruthless blue Mexican sky, men with horses and guns shooting at each other, paintings of jungles and beaches with almost no houses, and everywhere parrots. The first thing she noticed was how much fruit there was, the second thing how much gold. The first thing he noticed was how all the paintings of Angels looked like very real, very experienced young women, the second thing was that some of them were by no means white, in fact most of them were a sort of yellowish brown. Was it the varnish or a touch of the tar brush? Why shouldn't angels look like that, he thought, before he remembered that they hadn't come to look at Angels. They turned and walked smack into what they had come to see. A group of twelve small luminous paintings, the separate little wooden panels set within a single ornate frame, which threw its soft red-gold light around the spaces between the paintings. The first painting that caught her eye nearly knocked the wind out of her. She turned her back on it, with fists clenched and bending her head down, she said:

'Jesus, look at that hat. Describe it to me, what do you see?'

He puts on a terrifyingly accurate Stephen Hawking type voice, the sound of mechanically generated speech evolved for those with no other way of speaking. A sort of everyman/everywoman of a voice, a sort of neutered, disembowelled but bewilderingly portentous sound, which embodies everything that is most horrifically cynical about contemporary Western culture. Speaking though this mask of handicapped intelligence and suffering reason he says:

'There are many great mysteries in this world, and the human mind cannot but be drawn to confront them. But of all the riddles which lie before us, it is the riddle of life which is the greatest, and engages the first minds of all ages. I feel humble as I stare out from my wheelchair at these wondrous Mexican snapshots which explore nothing more and nothing less than the process of generation. Picture this if you dare, a staggering blue sky, with trees like swaying seaweed, or some primeval vegetation, stretched out across the azure void. In the foreground a round nosed very black woman, probably of Coromantin origin…'

At this point there is a slight pause, and then he goes on, in his own voice. The element of satire has gone, and there is an increasing urgency in his tone and something very like fear in his voice:

'She wears an elaborate blue silk head band, with rich gold embroidery. She holds out her hand, black against the blue sky. It's her right hand, the index finger is pointing, the three other fingers are half curled… The tip of her index finger appears to dissolve into the rich blue sky. She points across the head of a small brown girl, at a swarthy man with downcast features and an enormous broad brimmed hat. His face, partly because it is cast in shadow, carries an expression of smouldering hatred, perhaps even amused hatred, a hatred beyond reason and infinitely cruel. Whoever painted this thing knew about how much a man can hate a woman. The brown girl sits on his knee, clutching a large orange, looking out wizened and horrified at the unending sets of eyes which will stare at her and her parents over the centuries. She is gorgeously dressed in white lace chemise, a full, high waisted, aquamarine skirt, with gold and lace trimmings, and a white silk waistcoat, embroidered with fantastic flowers and birds. In the bottom right hand corner is a basket of exotic fruit, and enormous overripe seed pods. Several of the pieces are neatly cut, so that a missing section reveals a moist stone or seed. There is something obscenely intimate about their violent display, they look like human flesh, human interiors, they seem to hover somewhere between pornography and the operating table. Floating across the canvas at centre top the words 'De Espagñol y Negra: Mulata' the Spaniard and the Negress make a half caste. If you look carefully at the Spaniard's hat it is decorated with an enormous feather, the feather is coloured a preternatural electric blue, and is soft, like an ostrich plume. It is hard to make out definite forms, the feather is painted like smoke, but the last third of the feather appears, unmistakably, to have the form of a child, a naked new born child, a child completely unlike the brown child who sits between them. A little, electric blue baby, and its face has the same look as the man's.'

By this time she has recovered herself, and says:

'That's some description Dominic, you were on a roll, and that's some coincidence don't you think?'

'So that's cast painting.'

'How does it make you feel?'

'It makes me feel that people are definitely not fruit or vegetables. It's one hell of a way of saying that you don't always get what you want.'

PLAN

I

The young man in black with a red face and a sharp knife made a final cut. The string popped away and, like a gentle birth, a creamy fold of fresh papers slid out across the polished wood. A strong black hand picked one out. Two people went white as the sheet was held up. A woman walked off and coughed quietly behind a screen. A voice lisped, 'It could not be, so many people within so small a space'. Mirabeau, his palms resting on his temples, his fingers stroking the scant hair, thought 'a plan hides a body'. What he said to them was 'friends of the blacks, dine with me in six weeks and we shall see if it can be done'.

II

The carpenter arrived with a large wooden case. Inside was a beautiful frigate, one yard long, set upon a sea of frosted glass. On its stern was a brass plate with the word *Brookes* engraved upon it. The boat had no sails, and wasn't rigged. At one end, on a sort of raised platform, was a little brass cannon. The carpenter proudly touched a taper to the touch hole, and a small sharp explosion, the meaty smell of gun-powder, and a small hole in the plaster wall, caused Mirabeau to smile. He bent over the deck, saw the tiny brass hinges, and pressed a small lever near the cannon. Slowly the deck lifted, and below Mirabeau saw a scene of order and brilliant colour. The boat was an open shell, and the plastered sides were covered with burnished gold leaf. Small figures lay in rows on their sides, or their backs, all of them full length. Some were men, and some women, there were no children. They were painted all the colours of the rainbow.

A smell of fresh glue and paint had filled the room.

'Why all the colours' asked Mirabeau.

'I wanted to make them look happy' said the carpenter, taking a glass of deep, deep red wine, that was handed to him.

'The gold and silver may stay, but the figures must be black. Where did you learn to carve so well on this scale?' Mirabeau asked.

'I worked for the palace, I made ornamental carvings for the walls and ceilings, I made toys for their children. The Queen saw my work on a bathroom cabinet and asked me to make an ark for the Dauphin. I made the best of arks, they leant me the Encyclopaedia, huge books, some full of pictures, just pictures. I can't read, but there was a picture of the boat, sailing between lush banks of trees, and in another book, pictures of all the animals, every animal, animals I could not have imagined, so much difference.'

There was silence, and the smoke from the canon lay in strata against the rich curtains in the heavy air.

'I used the best cherry and pear wood, and a set of tools I borrowed from a friend who makes musical instruments. The finest chisels, and a graver that could make a mouse's eye, or a rat's teeth. I made them perfect, but I painted them all the colours of the rainbow.

Mirabeau picked up a figure, releasing the tiny shackle on its ankle, and smiling said:

'But these animals did not come in in pairs, you pious man, and their covenant may well be with the devil. I want you to paint them black, blue black, lamp black, the black of burned bones, I want you to paint their suffering.'

With a long agate nail Mirabeau picked at the teeth of the tiny little woman, now standing in his hand. Then he stowed her in her proper place, and softly replaced the deck, tears forced a passage out of his shut eyes, and shattered on the deck, some of the salt water fell onto the little bodies below.

III

The bottle was nearly empty, and standing next to an open book, with the name Athanasius Kirchner in heavy gold on the spine, a big man sat bolt upright. Mirabeau, his head held in his hands like a bowl of inestimable value, looked forward and muttered in an unstoppable rhythm like a prmitive motor:

'It should not really be that difficult, a problem of translation, they come from all over the place, but they are all Frenchman, and even some black ones, very soon some black citizens, and that will ease my task no doubt, get them up there to tell their story, tell a real story, we want them to have so much to say and they have no language to say it in, and too many tools to give them, the banality of fiction, the reiterations of narrative, the big shiny gift of our language, our entertainments, suck out more than they ever give, more than any workaday atrocity maybe has to offer, what is the point of dwelling on an obscenity, trying to enter into it, why enter into filth, you don't do that, you wipe it off, you get rid of it, bury it, you do away with it, you cannot think it through, alright, try and do that, do that filthy act, make yourself one with that horror, and what do you get into, what comes out of it, look at them writhing, look at them clinging to each other as if they were worms looking for an escape from the sun, just look at them, but we cannot, we cannot think it through, they are there, they cry, they shit, they starve, they cannot breathe, they get ill, they move this way and that, like maggots on a corpse, not enough light to see, not enough wind to feel, not enough air to breathe, see them, the near ones, climb on each other and scrabble and scramble, trying to get to something to breathe, see them cluster round the gratings, like grapes at a harvest. See it, behold it, look on, look on what you can never look on, there is no way of seeing it, yet I must make them see it. It must lie somewhere before me, it's a question of will to discover, well to rediscover, human experience is a series of repetitions there is no unique horror, there is no new situation that transforms us, there is no special space of suffering, there is no privilege of suffering, that's the thing to cling on to with these damn sentimentalists hovering about, they will spoil us, they'll spoil everything, with their bubbling consciences. We need to get away from this corrosive empathy, we need to do this to save our love of the black ones. We need to find out how to be there, how to get into their skins, how to flay ourselves. But the enormity of it, there is no language devised to explore such a reliving. I give it up.'

IV

The big speech had not been made. The dinner had been eaten, little speeches made, the black deputies from San Domingo, in electric blue, toasted. The young Englishman with a rare roast beef complexion and sheer black clothes had been thanked for his news and for his gift of engravings. Eighty people moved around the sideboard, long lines of little silver dishes carrying iced sherbets in pastel shades, coloured bon bons, and little biscuits, stood guard over the splendid boat, alone on its silent sea.

Mirabeau pressed the lever and said quietly, 'you now see how it can be done'.

As he spoke a stinking black boat lay in a harbour in Jamaica, and its hatches were removed so that tired sick black people could pull the well oiled remains of life from the blackness below. One man lay asleep, his arm draped over the stern, his index finger pointing with languid obliviousness directly at a large carved word. *Brookes*.

NEWTON

'I really think sir, for the good of yourself, and the decency of your congregation, you should desist, you should cease, from public sermons.'

Newton replied in a monotone: 'And shall the Old African Blasphemer cease while there is still breath in his body?'

Newton, a short, strong, fat man, shook his dewlaps, and gazed out sadly, for all the world like a small, muscular cow. Spittle hung from his jaw, and soaked into the starch of his cravat, reaching out across the flat whiteness in a damp grey stain, shaped like some soft unknown island, made of pure lead. The earnest voice continued:

'Sir your improprieties have disturbed the ladies, when you fell to raving about the hermaphrodite the ladies were distressed. Your oration upon the wickedness of all, upon the sacred stain of blood with which the Saviour soaked us all, even on the children, your fury at their inevitable mendacity, and the need to follow the straight path, no matter the cost, no matter the pain, frightened the ladies, the mothers, sir, the mothers with children.'

But the eyes of the old man had suddenly gone. Newton and his eyes had parted company, the eyes were over fifty years off, the surf breaking on the African coast, and a ship drawing anchor, about to sail.

Down in the cabin he was writing, willing his love to Mary in long sentences which wrapped up the gift bestowed on them. The sentence he was writing: 'My dearest Mary, God's protection of me was manifested yesterday in the miraculous discovery of an horrible plot...' There was a knock at the door, and a sailor reported, 'The most likely of the boys is on deck Sir'. Newton nodded and walked down the deck to where a small boy, bending slowly down and up, down and up, was lashed to a grating by the legs and lower body. Newton, four yards away, said quietly, but in a voice which carried admirably:

'How many grown ups wanted to kill me?'

The little black boy fixed his eyes on a brownish green mark, concave, on the sweating forehead, so that he would not have to look at the running eyes. His head was swimming, his hands tied together tightly and held out in front of him. Newton moved his lips an inch from the boys, and without seeming to draw breath continued in the same voice:

'How many grown ups wanted to kill me, what were their names, help me in God's work, help me in God's name?'

The five year old black boy wanted to stretch out his arms, to gesture as wide as possible, to tell this person the truth. The whole world of grown ups wanted to kill this ghost in stinking cloths, this grey figure, grey, fat. It was no good. If he had been able to stretch out his hands, and arms to suggest that everyone, everyone and everything he loved, wanted to kill the grey ones, all he would have done would have been to offer an embrace to the world. The short heavy man, with the white horsehair contraption on his head, moved off down the deck. Talking under his breath he intoned:

> Alas! by nature how deprav'd,
>   How prone to ev'ry ill!
> Our lives to Satan how enslav'd,
>   How obstinate our will!

Down in his cabin he carefully took out a small velvet case, slipped it in his breeches pocket, and wandered back, the words floating out across the waves:

> And can such sinners be restor'd,
>   Such rebels reconcil'd!
> Can grace itself the means afford
>   To make a foe a child?

When he returned to the boy Newton was carrying a small metal object, a part of a bigger whole, some bit of a great engine, or the works of a vast clock perhaps, so perfectly made. It was a thing of beauty, two small loops of steel, set vertically in a thin steel lozenge, another steel plate dropped over the loops, and then a central screw, with a small key to tighten it. The boy's thumbs were slipped into the loops, and as the Captain turned the little metal screw a noise began to come out of the boys mouth, a gentle hiss, like that a baby crocodile makes on emerging from the shell. Certainly not a human sound, this sound of a useless pain, caused by a useless violence.

There was nothing to tell, and no way of telling it. The Captain saw this immediately, he also knew how unpredictably half a turn too much could explode the knuckle joints. A child that couldn't do anything was food for fish. He removed the screws, and the little hands were perfectly unharmed. He looked into the boys eyes and saw a wild terror, where before there had been confusion only. The terror must grow, the wildness must go, the Captain thought. But he also thought out loud, 'These things take time, and that isn't my problem'. He ordered a drink for the boy, and thanked him for his co-operation. As the little naked shanks moved off up the deck, to be put under the sail tent where the women sat nursing babies, Newton scratched in his notebook. 'The children interrogated, clearly knew nothing, put one lightly in the screws to urge him to a full confession, he clearly knew nothing. God has protected us this voyage, and perhaps it is an infamy to require an account of the plot and the leaders, God knows and God protects. I will let the matter drop with flogging. Today I made a foe a child.'

BOX

I didn't like it, I wanted to go on my own. Three years I waited, three years watching Ruth and her horses, her own horse, a different horse every year. Always white, always Arabs, or something almost white with a lot of Arab in it. I would kill for an animal like that. It took three days by wagon to get in from the farm, along roads that weren't often roads but just fields of dirt, with a polished trail worn through the middle, like a snail or a slug or something had just been there. The end of summer and dust was caking the mule's ears. The mule was funny, it stood still lifting its front leg as if to stop someone hitting it , but when it moved its legs quickly across its head it was like an otter I saw once, eating a fish as if it was washing its face. I never saw anything like it, the mule was strong but stiff, a world away from the Arab I was going to meet, my horse, with a neck like a swan. You could die for the love of it, everyone knows they are cleverer than people, they see more, they know more, that's one thing Ruth and I agree about, about horses, they are kind things, kind and strong, bigger kinder and stronger than people, even than dad.

At the station there was a crowd, waiting to see my Arab. News gets about about a thing like that, and I expect dad wanted it to get about spending that much money on something that beautiful, don't say I don't feel guilty, I do feel guilty, but the way I look at it doesn't make sense anyway, because you never buy something that beautiful, you pay money to be allowed to look after it, just to be able to look at it, that's what dad always says about my mother, he's gallant.

We tried to get through the crowd to the big box, that must be in the freight car somewhere, but they were lifting all the other things out first. I thought I could hear breathing, beautiful deep breaths, but distressed, like he was distressed. I started to panic, to pull at my dad's coat, I screamed in a high voice. Dad tried to calm me, but I couldn't stop, I wasn't myself, I pushed into the crowd, and was still, they hadn't cared for the horse, maybe he was damaged. I stopped in front of a large box, on its side and about twenty of them, or more, round it. The breathing was still coming out, but it wasn't my horse any more, the box was too small, too small by half. I stopped crying, I was too sad to scream, I knew my Arab was dead now, but in pieces, they cut it up and made it into meat, and put ice on it, in the box, they do that with dead bodies, animals they cut up and put them in boxes, put them in boxes.

I knew my face had gone funny, the way dad was looking at me. He put his arms round me, lifted me up and told me to watch. He said watch, and you will see something incredible, a black man climbing out of a box, they say he travelled a thousand miles in it. They were in their shirt sleeves now, three of them, and I knew something horrible was going to happen, they stood about the box with claw hammers, working hard and sweating, the long nails came out of the wood each one with a different voice, the voices of pain, of dryness. Then one of them said, 'All right inside?', and a deep voice called out 'All right'. They lifted the lid off and two black hands with pink nails gripped over onto the sides of the box, and a fat black man sat up, in a white shirt, and he started shouting, in his deep voice about praise the Lord and suffering, and all sorts of stuff, and he really lost it performing like he was in the theatre, or mad or just didn't care any more. I could hear the neighing of a horse in the background, and in the gloom, inside the car, I saw him moving, like a big white rectangle, moving in and out of light, the sun and shadow of the slats, in and out of light, he was nosing the slats. My dad carried me to his box, I felt his head, I felt his ears and nose. I loved him to death.

CINDERS

When my father died he was cremated. And right through the service, as my older sisters stood there and nodded their tears, and my younger brother stood there, and my older brother stood there and managed not to cry as he read out a miserable poem, and the overblown sermon was spoken in weighty words by the wiry little, dark little, vicar, I could only think of one thing… fucking women. Not 'fucking women' in general, not, sort of women drivers sort of thing, but really fucking women, two in particular who I had not and who there was not much earthly chance I would, and I have to say I have serious doubts about the hereafter, although I hope it comes up trumps. Then I thought it's an odd way of putting it after what, where's here, but the poor old man wasn't here or there after he died, he was exactly in front of me in a box, under ground, out of my sight, in a coffin, below me, ahead of me. They were keeping him down there until he was going to rise up through the floor like a ridiculous jack in the box that never came out of the box, like a Lazarus that had blown it, got the timing wrong and really gone and died, he hadn't risen up to slide into the boilers yet, but I knew he was there, wait for it, wait for it, we were all thinking. But then I got to thinking of my lost opportunities, as I could not stop my mind from doing, they were both what I thought I wanted, on the outside and for all I know on the inside too, one was blond and one was black, the blond one was about thirty and had three children, the other one was young and dark and very thin, but with a bum that ran around in my mind, suspended as it was between something adolescent and something not, what a bum. I don't know why, at this juncture, at this turning point, as the fires were being started up for the person who had fucked with my mother to make me, I thought of these two women, both of whom I liked, and loved in a concerned kind of way, interest-in-what-they-had-to-say, softness-just-being-around-their-trust, and respect kind of way, I did respect them, I had never lusted after them, they trusted me, not if they read this, but they did, they viewed me almost as a sister.

My mind flickered between the one and the other, and as the music started I saw them wearing long hockey shirts, perfect quarters of crisp black and white, crisp cotton, and nothing else, bending over a smooth polar-white washing machine, turning their heads back over their shoulders and smiling. Then the dark one lifted the shirt slowly, very slowly, so that I saw the top of her legs, I knew they were smooth and bare. On top of the washing machine was a large bowl of blue glass, that lovely blue like a stained glass window, and inside it a selection of fruit and veg. She took a carrot, and then the blond one took it from her and put it back in the bowl, and then they both laughed over their shoulders at me. Why did I see that then?

Some nice music was playing – Schubert, Beethoven, Mozart, Schuman – my mind wasn't on the music but the fading carrot. My mother squeezed my arm at this point and my other brother began crying. It's a dark thing to watch a grown man cry, it's like watching a crime, a grown up giving up, and then a man, and to see that chin pucker, like a babes bum, and to see the spasms in that lower lip. I love this person, and he moved me deeply, his sorrow brought tears to my eyes, but I thought, he looks so ridiculous right now it would totally disgust me, if I were a stranger looking in on from the outside, so to speak, if I were disconnected from what was going on. The tears, have started coming and somehow that saves him and me, why does it take men so long to start crying tears? But they don't just come, they spurt, tears are jettisoned, shot out by some underground pressure, relief perhaps, it looks like a malfunction, and all I think about is that bizarre effect of looking through the back rear view mirror of my car, and when you press the button for the rear wiper it sends a crescendo of water spraying over the top of the car.

Well the fires started up again, and I had lost the train of my thought, again, my poor old younger brother, crying, moving that lower lip just like he had no teeth and was trying to chew up a bit of a vegetable, we're not cut out for that sort of thing any more I reckon, but at least it kept my mind off those two women, because I was starting to find the whole thing seriously distasteful, it's not like I usually spend my time day dreaming about women I really like, who are my friends, in that kind of suggestive way. But back to the point, here the back of my brother's chin had salt water running down it, he should have been bawling but he wasn't he was choking, really choking, I don't like to labour a point but he wasn't crying he was labouring through his sorrow, like he was giving birth to his tears or something, and the tears were coming slowly now, like an open wound, like they were seeping out from the fat veins of his sorrow, and all I could do, was to look at what happened to the skin, how it got darker and darker where the tears had gone down, like watering the earth or something. Like a stream through the parched land.

Then up it came, the box, with the last earthly remains of the poor old sod in it, and it starts moving along, smoothly, slowly, and all I can think of is a pile of groceries at the supermarket, slowly moving towards the check out, the doors opened and off he went into the gas fire, British gas I should expect, ashes to ashes. And I thought of a life of thoughts and love and hate and everything, book learning and experiences, wiped out, but mostly the hate, which had filled up most of the last third of his life. And I thought that cremation is a withering thing, because when your skin and flesh are gone you've got your bones, you've got a skeleton and it's always white, bone white, except for the fillings in your teeth, this incredible hard white set of bones, every one perfect in its place like a dinner service. We've all got a skeleton, why burn it? So when we saw then, in this metal tub, like some special offer biscuit tin or something, this soil stuff, I felt robbed. They weren't really ashes they were cinders, like something you clean out of a hearth, ashes would have been more dusty, finer, like white pepper. These were not, they weren't anything. They were lumpy like Bisto, but grey, grey grey. There they were his cinders.

KIDS

Tim was always the same. Soon as I met him we had a secret, because I was twelve, and I really loved him.

If you press your eyes they go blind for a bit. If you press them gently with your fingers, a bit, if you keep on pressing, like squeezing a trigger but didn't want it to go off, or like feeling a vegetable to see if it's ripe, and when you know it's ripe you go on feeling. I was doing that, and had caught the darkness out of light, and what I saw was like a dream. I saw this big swollen bag of rubbish, and if you kicked it, it all fell out, fresher and more alive than it had ever been before. Cans and paper wrappers on the cans, and on the plastic bottles, and on the sides of a lot of things, and banana skins and orange peel, and soft coffee and tea grounds, and this and that from everywhere, and cigarette ends, a million, all different, some with lipstick, some dry with lipstick still on them, some soggy and drowned, but you could still see they were butt ends, still separate, still themselves.

Then Tim asked me was I all right. I said to Fuck Off. I was startled. I didn't know Tim. But he stood there and said 'Are you all right' with a big open mouth, loose lips, the black between uneven, like a blackberry.

Well I was really sad. And I looked at Tim and he was sad too, but he was angry. I didn't know if he was angry at me, or angry sad, or always angry. Then Tim said that I looked like I wanted to hurt someone, and who was it? I said it wasn't him, but that I did. He said he'd been watching me for a long time and he knew it, so if I wanted to hurt someone today he could sort it. Tim wasn't tall, but he had a black face, and very baggy black trousers, they make everyone look the same, Kal my sister says they're like baby clothes, the clothes they wear on the streets.

When we got to the place Tim said to look over there. I looked at this poor old fuck, lying there. They were caked up and working to turn over a bit. But not really moaning, hissing more, the way a little cat does, that can't breathe easily, held up near your face. They were choked up, caked up, with this stuff on them, the place was such a tip, a shit heap. I couldn't tell you if it was blood or just their own filth, but someone had done the dirty on them.

I asked Tim if he had done that, 'It's just a toy, he said'.

When we left the house I went home. There was never much else to do. I don't know Tim, I don't know why. You can't leave old people alone, they're helpless, but they're not like kids, there's no way they're ever like kids. I thought of saying it to Tim, but what I said to myself was. I don't know why. You can't leave old people alone. They're not like kids.

T-POT

Tilted at an angle of forty five degrees, his right arm holding a big kettle, pouring a cup of tea, this heavy man, called T-pot, called out 'Who wants a cup of tea'. They didn't always call him T-pot just because he made tea for everyone, he did do that, and he poured it out. It's a chicken and egg question, unless you knew T-pot. They called him T-pot for a number of reasons. Do you want me to tell you? Why not. It's still a chicken and egg question. I can tell you how he first got hold of the name.

They called him Pot once, because when he was twenty he was fat, and we all ran around playing games, he had this pot stuck onto his belly, a piece of fat, exactly like a pot. Pot was a brick short, several, he was as thick as two shorts, daffy, but he would always come up with some words, some gibberish or other, sometimes he was funny but more often he was daft he would just let any old crap run straight out from his head along his tongue out into the world, it could really piss people off. He would say the stupidest stuff. Indignity that's what did for him, no matter what he said, and to be honest his talk was running out of control like his body, we could not see that sort of fatness as an achievement, an asset, we never thought of him as some kind of a business man, or a potentate, or a pasha, or a Buddha in the making or something. He used to sit there, with this bulge coming out through these big coloured T-shirts, and he used to always want to have the last word. And that's sort of where the tea came in. We knew a girl once, called Sally Putt, who worked in a caf, and always asked:

'Are you a mif or a mil, milk in first or milk in last?'

So one day T-pot starts on his usual bullshit, and starts asking her questions, and says, in this kind of nasty soft way:

'Why do you always ask that question?'

And he just won't let it go, and asked her:

'Why don't you say, one day, are you a tif or til?'

And I say, because this is T-pot stamping down some seriously sacred territory in the caf, and T-pot is in serious danger of dissing Sal:

'For Christ sake shut up, big mouth strikes again.'

But that was my mistake, Sal never needed anyone's help and the idea that she did is going to have bad results, and she tells me to shut the fuck up, and Sal says to him, with the danger signals in her eyes:

'Only a fucking git would ask a question like that.'

T-pot was a prat, and I can't warn him any more, so he says:

'There are no questions like that , there is the question and the opposite of the question, or as Bart Simpson says, there are no stupid questions just stupid people.'

She just pours the lot over his head, and the tea part is pretty damn hot and then when it's all running off of him she says:

'This is the Pot of Tea which you have asked for and here is the fucking milk, now shut the fuck up you boiled black bastard, mix it anyways you like you'll still be a pot bellied black bastard with tea running down your pot belly.'

T-pot sat there with the tea dripping down his shirt, he had the wet look all right with the shirt sticking to the fat, and she was so pissed off, and we were wetting ourselves, and then he just starts crying, very quietly. The weird thing is that a load of water is just running out of his eyes like there was a leak inside his head somewhere. I never saw anything like it. But, as we all said, he had it coming, he never did know when to put a sock in it, and someone had to tell him to shut the fuck up. But then, as we all know, that is one of life's common problems.

END OF THE LEG

I

They were just lying there on the grass, looking so old and sticky. I thought, well that's a nice thing to come across on a Sunday lunch time. Then Elsa said:

'Why don't you, if you fancy it, why don't you pick them up?'

And then we laughed, because it looked kind of ridiculous these bits of something that belonged to something else, or several things, we did not even recognise. There was one thing for sure, they weren't even human, but a kind of greenish milky white, like bits of a dead creature would be if they'd been lying around, cut off, on the grass all afternoon, kind of exactly the thing you don't expect to see really. It must have been hit by a car, what it or they belonged to once must have taken one hell of a whack from a car. Probably one of those big car trucks with a bull bar on the front, one of those big metal trucks, that people who live in little town houses often decide to buy. God only knows why, they're not going on safari, and when did a bull ever get hit by a bull bar, when did a bull even look at a bull bar? But certainly these things had been through the mincer.

Elsa and me looked at the stuff more closely, and there could be no doubt it, this was off some kind of a small creature, like a scrawny kind of a foot that could perhaps only belong to a very big bird or a really small albino fox, or a badger, or a giant stoat or cat or middle sized dog, a setter, the white feet off a liver and white spaniel. So then they would not have been feet at all, but paws, claws, hoofs, talons, or something along those lines, but then again they didn't have any fur or feathers, just this really thin skin, like the skin under fur or feathers, as if whatever was on top of them, had just been shaved off, really fine right down to the skin.

Well we picked it all up and put it in a Tesco bag, with all these red white and blue stripes, a kind of Union Jack gone through the mincer, a joyful bag, or as Elsa said at the time:

'Put it in the flag-bag.'

I was cycling back with it, it was put in the back of the bike, I didn't have a basket just a child's seat, dirty white plastic, someone told me that people don't steal bike's with children's seats so I had one fitted, a dirty trick really, playing on people's sympathy. As I put the bag down one of them slid out, and it was definitely the foot of a child. Call the police.

II

Well we got there early and they were already pretty drunk, Janet and I knew they were a dodgy couple, I mean designer dykes are all right, but they seemed to be in some secret pact to take the piss all the time and the pact, or was it a conspiracy, was fuelled on Chablis. Why we kept on going I don't know, I really don't know. The last couple of times we had gone round there they had got steadily more pissed and more and more outrageous, really, well not outrageous, just boring, I mean they were just trying to shock everyone, and Janet in particular, but they had a damn good shot at it, until we called their bluff. Well they knew Janet was a vegan, and I mean that not eating meat was a central focus of her life, I mean central focus as in a religion, sort of macrobiotic fixation on not being contaminated with living things, apart from vegetables. Well they brought in a beautiful dish, a glass dish from Murano, they said they had had it ordered to their own design, and watched it being hand blown, or mouth blown I suppose, or mouth and hand blown to be totally accurate. They had it filled with these beautiful crispy light green things, with little fringes, sort of aquatic looking like seaweed popcorn. And Janet was raising her fingers to her mouth when one of them, Elsa I think, blurted out:

'Don't eat it you carnivorous cannibalistic vegetarian.'

And they looked at each other and guffawed, Jesus they looked like two donkeys saluting the dawn. Clearly a windup, we thought, but what can you do, you can't take chances on this stuff, or I couldn't, the fallout would have been just too much. So we both said, in chorus like a Greek tragedy:

'What do you mean?'

Then Elsa says to Janet:

'Would you eat a carnivorous plant?'

And after the pause she's expecting she goes on:

'Well that's stir fry Venus fly trap, now they are young ones, but so what, there will be a lot of little flies that were digested, and they have gone to make the flesh of that plant, now this is a test case, animal, vegetable, mineral?'

Then Janet, whose so used to arguing that she always steps back to at least three stages before says:

'What's that got to do with cannibalism?'

And Elsa says:

'Read about it, I have, it's been filmed and noted, if a piece falls off one of those plants into the jaws of another open piece, the plant mouth bit that catches it, eats it, it's a reflex action, like a very slow motion of a Shark in a feeding frenzy, it eats its own kind, but its own kind is made up of the flesh and blood of flies. That's vegetarian cannibalistic carnivoraciousnesh.'

Her enthusiasm bleeds the last syllable out into the Chablis a little too long, but still its a good windup, and even when Elsa insists that the stuff is really cleverly disguised mange tout, we still have the jitters, and the evening takes a long time to pick up.

So that's what I am talking about, that's a flash guide to the history of their efforts to anger us, so on this night in question we get in there, and the two of them are really slaughtered. They start looking at us askew and giggling, and then they say that they have cooked us up something really special. Its a cleverly disguised vegetarian version of jugged hare. So Janet says:

'Why bother, it's a sick idea to take the most gamey and carnivorous cliché you can think of, the kind of thing that only farting old dons stick down their necks, and to make a parody of it.'

And Elsa says:

'It's taking things the way they've been going for a very long time, look in every damn supermarket freezer and its groaning with veggie burgers, and veggie sausages, and veggie parodies of carnivorous junk food, so why not do the mimicry with some style, and go for something that Samuel Pepys might have eaten and farted out.'

And then Elsa says:

'I had a brain wave, to combine jugged hare with calves feet in jelly, to provide a sort of double whammy parody. I feel that it will cement our friendship, make or break.'

By this time we are all completely rat arsed, and I just totally don't really give a toss actually, because we are getting desperately hungry, because this kind of bullshit of theirs always holds the actual meal up until about nine o'clock, so what are we supposed to do? So I say in my John Wayne/Robert Mitchum voice:

'Hell babe, cut the shit, roll out them wagons, give me some covering fire, and russel up some grunts out there on that goddam table.'

So they do, and there is this big fat heavy blue French enamel designer casserole and it's fuming with something lumpy and very meaty smelling inside it. And it's cooked black, it looks like tar and dumplings, or a piece cut out from a bog in Tipperary. It's so over the top that there is nothing that we can do except to start laughing and to eat it. Elsa, says it's Soya and thistle stalk hare's foot calve's jelly. And we all fall about laughing, the idea is just too, too grotesque. Well with organic mashed potato it tasted excellent, and when they told us that really it was child's foot, hare's foot, calve's jelly we completely lost it. Sometimes you've just got to laugh even if it is in bad taste, well you can't just walk away from it all the time.

RUNNING A BATH, HIS STORY

I went round there, sometimes. It was a dirty old house, and there was a dirty old woman who lived in it. Mrs. Foshon, she was called, but it was pronounced Focean, like Ocean, but it was even softer the way the words came softly out of her fat lips, they didn't exactly trip out, they oozed out, like someone who'd done badly in a fight, but still had like a bit of a fight in them. She had a face that was shaped like an old balloon, left hanging in a corner after a party, until it went all cellulite in a corner, until someone found it and really couldn't stand it any more so they took it away and stuck something sharp in it. Her face was just like the bottom of an old ashtray, one of those fat beige ash trays, with a transfer drawing of a village street on it, and then all those like little scrubbly bits of stale tobacco, and all those flakes of ash, black, charcoal grey, silver grey like an old person's hair, a rich one, browny slimy grey, all piled up, like a mass grave.

Mrs. Foshun wasn't too mobile, she never did much except for sitting in a huge wheelchair, next to an enormous boiler, that ran on coke Who uses coke any more, I mean like to light a fire, to keep warm and stuff? She doesn't walk, maybe she's a cripple, or paralysed, or just too heavy and got no muscles in her legs any more? Well she sits there in a huge gown, its a brownish green kind of gown, and there's a terrible sweet smell, like overripe fruit that drapes itself around everything. After you have left her place they come up and ask you what you've been doing to make yourself smell like that? I just don't answer questions like that, I tell them to take a walk. Well, like I say, she never really moves about much, she sits in the chair, which has all these bald greasy spots on its arms, and the bare wood poking through like a skeleton through a raggedy body…and I bring her in huge buckets of coal, I mean coke, which I can hardly lug around, they virtually really do my back in to drag to her. Then she hoists the buckets up and over over the counter at which she sits, with a huge swelling yellow arm, grunting softly like someone has punched her right in the gut. And she gets her poker, a really big metal pole, and she stirs up the fire, and the yellow arm going like a blancmange, and then when it's hissing white hot, the fire that is, she pours half a ton of this coke on, and it hisses back and then on I go. It's really a drag, and she's really weird, all she does all day is to sit there in front of the hot hot fire, and the stove is glowing, in the dark, like one of those glubby lamps. She really smells a bit, but not really like I would if I were like sitting there in front of the old hissing stove that's giving off fumes like a burger grill. And all she ever seems to have on the counter is some really huge oranges, oranges as big as mellons or balloons, and she rolls them around in the green light, with her big smooth yellow hands. She doesn't even seem to sweat, there's a bit of a sheen or something on her skin, and her long grey straggly hair, which she greases off of her face sometimes with this amazingly fat hand. One hand is twice as fat as the other, like that's why the kids call her banana fingers, or that's one of the names I've heard when I take her out.

Foshun keeps huge piles of money, piled up on a table. There was this one little pile and it's all round bright gold, mint new coins, and I just slipped three in my pocket, because I was in the front room, and Foshun, and her boiler and her oranges and stuff are in the back room, and the door is only open a crack. Well the next time I come to see her she has this really like glarey look in her eye, and she says:

'You know my little round table?'

And I say:

'Yes.'

And she says:

'Well you know there is lots of change piled up on that table?'

And I say:

'Yes.'

And she says:

'Well there are three gold coins missing from my little pile of bright ones, do you think you could have a look for them for me?'

And I say:

'Yes of course, Mrs. Foshun.'

And I climb about on the floor on my hands and knees, smiling like a cat and swearing to myself. I know that there is no way in the world I will find these coins because I have eaten them about two days ago, when I bought me and my friends a load of sweets. So I go back to Mrs. Foshun, and I say I looked all around and see no sign of the money, no sign at all. But she's smiling too, and then she really shocks me when she says:

'Now go upstairs and clean the bath.'

Well Foshun has never asked me to go up her manky stairs before. She's never let me into any room except the front room and the place where she sits, which I call the boiler room. I didn't know she had a bath, and then she says:

'The Ajax is in the cupboard in the bathroom, and the sponge is there too, wash it with cold water, then fill the bath up to one third with warm and give the ring a good going over.'

I simply do not know what Ajax is. It must be some kind of like soap, and been sitting in the cupboard since before they invented electricity. I try to imagine what its going to look like, and to feel like, and to smell like, and I can't, just call a blank. Then I see a big cardboard box with faded beautiful colours on it, and maybe a picture of some woman, in one of those pleated skirts, like a scallop shell, holding a cloth with the Ajax, which is glowing green like a caterpillar… maybe that's what Ajax is like…

Well I don't have a choice do I, no choice at all, I could walk out of the place but that would be like saying I was guilty. Anyway the only way out, seeing as there is a huge red curtain nailed up over the inside of the front door, is straight out past Foshun and her boiler. I'm just not up for that one, she is just too scary. So up I go and there is a huge bath, grey iron on the outside, and a horrible set of yellows inside like something that leaked out of a blister, and there were soft sort of stringy things growing on the side that looked like white sausages, and I feel ill. You needed a spade, or a road drill, or a strimmer, to clean out this stuff, or some strong weed killer or something, like the stuff a psycho would put in the bath to dissolve a corpse. Then a really terrible thought hits me behind the head, and I start sweating, yes you know what I'm thinking. And the fruit smell is really ripe. This must be it's home, or it's breeding ground. The bath must have been here a long time I think, longer than Foshun, and that means that it had other people in it before her huge backside was lowered into it. So if I concentrate on those things it might all get better. I might be able to think of a history of some sort, or something to take my mind off things being murdered and cut up and dissolved and stuff.

Well I'm telling you this because I know something here is not quite right, I know Foshun's up to something. And I hear her moving and creaking around downstairs, and she shouts:

'Turn the taps on, won't you?'

And me I don't say anything.

So I grab a tap and I start turning it round, and round. It's a bit difficult, because when you get half way round a turn it starts gripping and making this groaning scraping sound like there's some sand or broken glass or something in there, or something really in pain or being tortured. The handle starts really digging into the palm of my hand. And then there's a rattling sound, and the water comes out, and its a nasty pinkish greyish colour, like rust mixed with snot. I sit down on a bathroom stool that's powder blue wicker, blue like a packet of French cigarettes, and I start thinking I would really like a cigarette. Then I hear a creaking and groaning sound, and heavy breathing, like someone's on a life support machine. Before I know it she's in the doorway, it's impossible but she's levered herself up the stairs, and she's the closest thing I ever saw to actually standing up. She's really breathing, and it makes the tops of her huge yellow arms move up and down like sea beasts or anacondas or an earthquake. I feel the hairs rise all over my body in a burning sensation. She stares at me through her yellow eyes and she says:

'Get out.'

And I say,

'Don't you want me to get the Ajax?'

And I say this, not because I am shit scared, which I am, and trying to please her, which I am, but really because now my curiosity is up and I'm dying, completely dying, to know what this Ajax stuff looks like. But she just says:

'No, I made a mistake, you can go now, take a walk.'

And I am turning to go, and she's sitting on the edge of the bath with her great big greasy gown round her great big greasy body. I don't know if it's a trick of the light or what, with the sun going down through a window. What I see is her lift her leg and like put a big thick ankle in the water. Her ankle is more like most people's neck, and her foot is more like an animal's head, like an upside down sheep's head. The water is bright red, really thick oily bright red, and her foot goes in, and her ankle, and it turns bright red, like tomato ketchup. I hear her let out a terrible groan, not a human sound, or if it is a human sound then its the kind of sound at the end of your life, or having an orgasm, something pretty final. And I walk down the stairs, and out.

Well I only went back to see Foshun the one more time after that. She's sitting in her big chair, and the boiler's hissing and shimmering, and the sun's out, and it's very hard to see her in there.

'I've come to get my money.'

I say, and she says:

'I think we both know what you mean.'

And I don't say anything.

She looks with her huge hand in the draw, and gets out a dirty old piece of paper, and she wraps up a dirty crumpled fiver in the paper. I can't take the money without the paper so I take them both. I look with the light of the boiler spilling out like a sunset, and her whole body is like a cooked lobster, and she looks at me with the heat of the fire falling full on the side of her face. There's mark on it, the colour of beetroot, like a birthmark. Then she turns to me and she smiles, and it's a really sweet smile, like a baby.

Out in the dusk I unwrap the fiver. There is an address on the paper, Malin Street, Liverpool 1, and the name of a photographer, and then it says, Miss Norris and Mr. Foshun, no. 45. And I turn it over and it's actually a photograph, and it's an old style wedding photograph, down on the Albert dock. There they are, all standing underneath a huge crane. A crowd of black people and lots of white people laughing, with the grey water spread out like polly filler. Miss Norris is there with the same smile I just saw on her face, looking straight through the camera at me.

PICTURE WINDOW

I

When did I first see it? Maybe if I knew that I'd be reading my own mail again. I can't remember when I first saw it. That might be why it's not possible to see it clearly now. But it wasn't all my fault, part of the problem was that they could not see me for wat I was. Really they were always as blind as bats, or moles, no worms, they were stone blind, pitch black blind, like worms, just feeling, and eating, eating into you, chewing, just being nasty, polished maggots, like white agate, or yellow like ivory, at first I thought they couldn't help it, but I was wrong they turned themselves into worms, just nasty.

II

You see in this modern world no one likes a real man, a real, in your face, fecund, big balled, and fertile male. A person who sees himself, in the end, or at least at his end, as the a great inseminator, germinator, *pater familias*, a big daddy. And it feeds into all of us, this desire to procreate, this knowledge that you have the capacity to fertilise every woman on the planet several times over, millions of times over. Each man, if he but knew it, could generate enough sperm in a lifetime to do God knows what, I mean think about it, three ejaculations a day, every day of your life, from the age of fourteen, or twelve, or whenever you start being a potential father. That's an awful lot of sperms. No wonder we are a driven breed, a violent gender, what with all that frustrated potential. A breed driven on by seed. What a waste, what a criminal waste, had we but world enough and time, if every man could really let rip. What a thought. So that was the problem, my male drive. It led me up blind alleys, it made me unpopular. I can tell you, and I will tell you. I kept asking questions, I was new at the job and it was all a bit bewildering. Simple questions at first, whenever they told me to do something. Then, I asked the questions, at the beginning, a long time before I got round to the idea that maybe, just maybe this little laddy was going to stop asking little questions and give them one great big answer. Not always out loud, but I asked them. Why shouldn't I? And the questions were all around why they worked us so hard, and like why I had to do it now. About why we all did, really, about why they or anyone did. Well we did, and did. But they noted it down, I was a trouble maker, they thought I couldn't keep my mind on it, but really I couln't keep my mind off it, I couldn't think about anything else, like a rabbit on a wheel, or a hampster. Goosey fucking gander, upstairs and downstairs, but never a sniff of my lady's chamber. It wasn't easy to concentrate, when you could only think about the one thing. Rivers of sperm boiling over and going to waste, maybe never even spawned, hold on to that picture. Thinking about one thing all the time is like not thinking at all, after a time. I tried to have it out with them, I tried to reason, I tried to be reasonable, but they scuttled off, crawled off, didn't want to know, in fact could not care less, if you put a cannon against their head and said, care, or I'll shoot, they couln't have thought how to care. They wouldn't listen, lend me their ears, they wouldn't face up to me, look me in the eye, look at me, to be honest they wouldn't give me the time of day, not that I ever asked them, I wasn't allowed to ask them, they wouldn't have liked it, maybe I should have asked them, how would I know they wouldn't like it if they never were asked, and I wanted to do things they never liked, I wanted to do things they positively hated. But they stifle you, you don't know right from wrong in the end, which end it might be, black from white, night from day, happy from sad, work from play, good from bad, light from dark, girl from boy, man from woman, male from female, top from bottom a hole from a pole. Why do they think I was born with two testicles swinging in my boxer shorts, just to sit there and whistle to the wind? I had to do something about it, but I needed the money, we all did. I had to do something about it, but I needed the nerve, I was always nervy, but I didn't have the nerve to do anything, that's the way it goes. But something has to give, you can't go on like that, day in day out, sleepless nights in the attic, thinking about nothing, because there is only the one thing to think about, and as I said, if you think about the same thing all the time, that's not thinking, that's not even living, breathing. In the end you have to do something, you can't just go under, because they scuttle off, and then put you in the shit, you can't. In the end it all gets used up, you feel diddled, like you've been diddled, short changed in the most brazen way, you've got to do something about it, face up to them, square up to them, hold up your dukes, be bold, give it a go, have a go, let them have it, have a dip, have a go, make your-self into a person again, fry them or fuck them, as Bruce Lee used to say. Otherwise what's the point, what is the point of it, if you're frightened all the time, but you don't know why, and they don't know why, but they try hard to frighten you, they don't know why, but they do it anyway, because they don't know, beyond their control. Are they frightened? Are they frightened because they frighten you or because someone else has told them to frighten you, or because they are frightened of someone who has been told to frighten them, to freeze their balls with terror, and someone else has frighened them, and so on and so on and so on, like some tedious philosopher on a telly show. Ridiculous really, but what can you do about it. It's ceaseless, really it goes on forever, if nothing happens for too long, you get frightened, because nothing happens, sooner or later it's got to change. You might just dry up – you might just forget what to do and how to do it, and why. It took a view to do it, I finally lifted my eyes up and had the courage, the bottle, to look out, I joined the navy, I saw the sea. I looked out of the window one day and I saw that the sun wasn't even shining, it wasn't raining either, just a perfect silver light, soft and luke warm and calm. It wasn't warm and it wasn't cold, it wasn't white and it wasn't black. Just a perfect day.

III

I was holding a very dirty letter at the time, and really that was what set it off, that was the touch paper. A message of two pages. I was holding my balls in one hand and a paper knife in the other. It was a nice thing, I had just bought it, the first act I had got round to doing in a long time. It had a little wooden scabbard and was a miniature Samurai sword, like Bruce Willis would have used. And one of them came up and asked me what I was doing, right up in my face, with their nose screwed up like a black rabbit, and they took off their glasses to scratch their nose, and I saw their naked eye ball. And that's when I stuck them like a pig. I was holding a very dirty letter at the time, and really that was what set it off, that was the touch paper. The letter simply said that you didn't do what they said you had to do. I looked down the lovely silver blade, one of them came up and asked me what I was doing, right up in my face, with their nose screwed up like a white rabbit, and they took off their glasses to scratch their nose, and I saw their naked eye ball. And that's when I slid the blade in as hard as I could, really quickly, first in one eye, and then, even before I started screaming, straight into the other one. Can you see the point of all this?

NAIL

Stop biting your nails, how many times have I heard it, what a load of crap. Sometimes, 'stop biting those nails', or 'I simply can't bear that sound', crap, biting my nails. I don't bite these pieces of ruined horn which grow out of my body, how can you say that, bite, I don't bite, I develop a friendship with my finger tips, with each one, through my teeth, a kind of shabby, on off, evolving relationship, with the finger and what's grown under it's ends, and what grows over it's ends. What difference does it make?

I once had a girlfriend tell me, she would bite them off for me, my finger nails that is. That she found seeing me bite them so 'traumatic', that was her word, traumatic, that was her stupid, over the top, word, that she would do the job herself. But would she know, how could anyone know, how could anyone understand who has rejected that intimacy with the points of your body that refuse to believe that they are either alive or dead. She had no right to claim a knowledge she had shed, or rejected, she was left out of this one, out in the cold, the stranger at the feast, and as always she didn't like it, not at all. The finger ends are, you see, the neap tide of our suffering tissue, that which is beyond a certain point – the point of pain. Can you put them beyond a point of no return, that is a thought we who sculpt our nails with our teeth always have. I remember when I first felt close to a horse, I hate horses, and I hate their long dirty yellow teeth, and their ridiculous huge gums, grinning at you like Fagin, and threatening to give you a nasty bloody nip at the very least, maybe a bloody great bite, a wound, but I remember when I first put all this aside and really felt for a horse. It was seeing a Western on a black and white television this man with a beard and nails bristling out of his mouth, I mean real nails that is because he was a blacksmith. Well he was banging some of these nails into a horse's foot and he missed with a nail, and the horse gave him this huge kick, like a firework going off, and my nails came to mind, and that was that. What's the point in this – hard to say, there isn't a lot of point in a finger nail. You don't acutally do that, bite your nails, you chew them, lick them, admire their softly altered and damaged forms, consider their ruined potential, and their horrible bloody minded, unalterable need to go on growing. Everything stops growing at some point, but not your nails, someone even told me they go on doing it when you are dead, your brain is gone, you are gone, but there they are, like eels in a sack, moving away slowly, for days, after you've left, is that growth, is that going anywhere, what is the point of that? But that's the point, and if I were to tell you that my hands were as black as the ace of spades and that is why I bite those pink nails out would it make any difference. And if I were to tell you that my hands were as white as milk and that is why I bite the pink nails out would that make any difference? Pink, pinker, pinkest, and at a certain point, if you bite on, if you bite hard enough, if you dare, the pink bleeds into blood, and blood is always red, they say it can be blue, but I never saw it.

Well that's why I do it, a sense of resentment, they're no part of me and I want no part of them, nip them in the bud, get in there first, cut them off in their prime, do it to them before they do it to you, nasty little buggers, shifting about between the living and the dead, between day and night, white and black – skin, horn cuticle, the sudden whiteness of detached layers, like onion skins upon a chopping block. The play of wet and dry, a tidal influence of sorts, serrated, belated, lick it, some of it goes pink again, retreats into something not thought of before, the way forward, the way back. Then beyond a certain limit the question of colour. Then before a certain question of colour there is the question of the end. Then before the question of the end there's the question of choice – the sucking of which finger when, and where do the thumbs come in – and then back again – where's there an end of it? Then the question of pain, does it hurt, doesn't it, is that why you do it, and if it hurts then it's you not that nasty little thing stuck on the end of you, the scab on the wound, the fairy on top of the christmas cake. It's a war I tell you, to try and drive them out, to try and stop this dead end growing, if that's the case then you just can't win, no way, so that even when you're dead they go on growing for a couple of days – dead eels in a sack moving, you can't win with that stuff – nerve endings – there's no end to it.

SPADE

Digging up a root, the spade hit a bone, a skull in fact, a human skull with a big hole in it. Bending down she picked up the skull and placed it carefully on a piece of old yellowing newspaper. Wind rustled the trees and autumn leaves began to fall. One leaf, picked out for the purpose, moved with a rocking motion through the air, like a baby being lulled to sleep, it came to rest on the skull, perfectly covering the hole in it.

The chances of that ever happening again must be zero she thought, despite the fact that she was still shocked at finding a skull.

Many years ago, a large girl was walking home when a strong hand was cupped brutally over her mouth, and a booted foot kicked her legs out from under her. A very long time after she had stopped screaming, and once they had all finished with her body, they threw it in a ditch. It was autumn, and the leaves began to fall. One leaf in particular fell through the air with a rocking motion, and was about to settle on the tip of the yellow girl's nose when a sudden gust of wind carried it on.

These foolish things, these foolish things, these foolish things.

COLOURS

A college feast is a tedious affair, one usually spends the majority of one's time worrying about being stuck next to the most crashingly tedious of our older fellows. One's left with nothing to say and very little way of saying it, one is snuffed out by their mean spirited cantankerousness. If I were being completely candid I might be inclined to think that a lifetime with these marsupials has ruined my mind. These feast affairs are nothing short of beastly. The most one can hope for is to be in some sort of proximity to the only young don's wife with a decent pair of breasts to hang out to air. A sad confession indeed but unfortunately true. So when I saw the seating plan, I was, I suppose, really quite deeply excited.

It hardly needs to be emphasised that it is not often that the opportunity presents itself for one to be seated next to a genuinely intriguing individual. I was to be placed beside a man who had done strange, if not in the opinion of many, entirely admirable, things with his life. It was altogether an unexpected bonus that this was an individual with whom I was not entirely unacquainted. I had indeed talked to him at length when I was in my early twenties, at a time when I still had some hefty ideas bubbling away, before fifty years of tutorial teaching ruined my intellect, indeed dried out my brain like a pretzel. He was then in his fifties and the older anthropologists were very suspicious of him. In fact no one in the faculty would pass the time of day with any civility, and consequently I grasped my opportunity with both hands, and would task him with questions at every opportunity. I must have appeared somewhat naive and presumptuous, but his generosity astounded me. It is exasperating to cast ones mind into the dark backward and abysm of time, the things of which I speak all happened a lifetime ago. People such as we then were, do not exist any more, and I may, in consequence, be guilty of speaking what is, to all intents and purposes, almost a foreign language, when I try to describe him to you and to recall the context for a story, which, now that I think about it, might be received as somewhat fantastical.

Trust me when I say that I am not sure how much of the story which I am about to tell I could reconstruct in his own inimitable manner. The question is, however, academic, in that a tape recording of his narrative exists somewhere within my personal archive, and when the time is ripe I will play it to you. If I cannot remember his words, in precise form, I can at least remember most vividly, what he looked like, and I suppose that I should try and describe him first, before that is, launching into a narrative of which at best I can claim a half memory. I might add, that I am not very good at this sort of thing but, but I would venture the phrase: 'a great big lumbering Australian' as an approximation of his likeness. Like so many of his countrymen he was an incurable traveller, and he loved to tell traveller's tales. It was in this context that he told me a story of which I never quite knew what to make. I never knew if the narrative was supposed to be taken with a pinch of salt, he ate a tremendous amount of salt, or whether it was quite simply truth, albeit embellished by the decorations of his peculiar prosody. He was a very odd kettle of fish, a genuine mixed bag, and although I was devoted to him, I might even venture the term genuinely fond, I never entirely trusted him. I hardly need to say that I intend no insult, I don't think I ever entirely trusted anyone or anything, the life I have lead did not necessarily require the introduction of such a concept. I certainly never needed to trust myself, effectually I had no responsibilities whatsoever, the life of a don is really rather like spending one's entire existence within a glorious playroom, with a good number of smaller children around to make things entertaining. I probably should not be saying any of this, I do not like talking about people, and I do not like talking to people, it gets to my nerves and makes me jabber. My years of sitting in my rooms with the silences widening between myself and some god-forsaken, gormless and saturnine undergraduate, who had failed to grasp the first principles of Etruscan political organisation or the like, have left me with a tendency to go on a bit, to go on so long that I put people off. But before I leave my 'lumbering Australian' behind, and get into the meat of the story, I really feel in all decency, that I should say a little about how enigmatic the man was.

I am not just making it up. What I really mean to say is that I never understood quite what made him tick. Maybe I say this because he was so chaotic in some ways, and so precisely ordered in others. Well of course at some level we quite simply all are, aren't we? If I repeat that phrase, that he was ordered in some ways and completely chaotic at the same time, then I could perhaps equally well apply them to myself, or to any number of individuals, you for example. Yet I am attempting to describe in as direct a manner as possible something quite out of the ordinary here. How can I put it, in a dramatic way? Everything was a performance, but imagine living one's life, when fate had constituted one in the form of a spectacularly undramatic individual, as some kind of a performance. The question which lies behind such a supposition being: what kind of a performance would it be, well really? That isn't to say that he didn't try to make painfully dramatic gestures, he was definitely larger than life. At some points, in terms of action, in terms of when he went where, and why he went there, he made his life into the most exotic of displays. The exasperating thing was the manner in which a gargantuan dullness sat at the back of it all, like an incubus on a naked virgin, or to put it more bluntly, and assuming that you will forgive the vulgarity of my simile because of the precision of the thought behind it, like a beer gut on a fashion model. He translated the kind of experiences most of us would have died to witness, let alone to endure, into a colourless matter, a putty-like sludge. I am not saying that I could have done any better, that would be, to put it mildly, presumptuous, how could I dream of implying such a thing, but it would not be inappropriate to infer that he let himself down, that on occasions he had been perceived to turn himself into something very close to a clown, or to put it in somewhat more portentous terms, he involuntarily parodied his own capacity for tragedy. When he came to remember, to tell us about, what he had done, or what he had seen, the shoes were crazily elongated, he didn't trip but launched into cart-wheeling somersets that were pure slapstick. But, as he knew better than most, when you let yourself down low enough it can be something of an eye opener for everyone concerned.

He was always passing through Europe on his way to one place or another. He had one of those peculiar and indeterminate research jobs in which the older universities specialise, and which have absolutely no rules attached to them, and, inevitably, not that much money either. He had enough to get by, but he was condemned to a life detached from what the majority of our population see as the normal sequences of adulthood: courtship, marriage, employment, not to mention the purchase of a house, and a car, the procreation of children and the appropriation of life insurance and pension schemes. He had no understanding of possessions, family, the various myths of permanency we all crave to live with, in order to convince ourselves, against all reason, that finally we are not alone and doomed to a certain, final, and usually painful, death.

Maybe he was the closest thing to a desert father that you could hope for these days, a Nazarene, a shaman, a seer, one of the wise ones. Mayhap because of this, his true nature as it were, his behaviour was shot through with a pernicious desire for engagement with the facts of low life. He possessed what amounted to a craving for finding out the dirtiest minor details about anyone and anything, and this propensity for nosiness, for sticking his proboscis into life's less salubrious nooks and crannies, stopped him, at least in his capacity as an anthropologist, from going the whole hog. True wisdom is big and clean, like a newly washed Bentley. He was condemned to live his life as a perpetual watchman, always on the lookout for the mechanisms which, in his world view, made people tick. What he failed to understand was that he needed to stand outside and admire, to get a sense of the whole picture, that in ultimate terms it was pointless to crawl about like some kind of inter-cultural mechanic, down in the guts of the machine. In regarding character as an approximation of a primitive steam engine, rather than as a late Titian, he might be accused of a certain tangentialism, as it were, not to say interpretative coarseness.

He shared, as with so many of those of us who choose the life of an intellectual, the tendency to think too much, and indeed too directly, about almost everything. Yet think as he might the severity of his training restricted his vision and he always saw things the same way, and translated his sight of them into the same language. Again, I might add, this may simply have been an illustration of an irritatingly frequent side effect of the intellectual conformity ultimately required by academe. He once informed me, in tones approaching enthusiasm, that he greatly prized an aphorism frequently upon the lips of his lisping old tutor. It ran, in essence, along the following lines: namely that there were only a certain number of thoughts which could be perfectly expressed in a certain number of words. The task of the intellectual was to achieve at least one perfect fit between thought and word in the course of one's writing career. Inevitably the early Pater and the late Henry James were held out as stylistic exempla. These queer fellows might be deemed unfortunate models for an aspiring cultural anthropologist of his inclinations, but don't let me get ahead of myself.

I would add, in order that I might pre-empt charges that my attitude exhibits an unfortunately forced superiority, that people in glass houses should not throw stones, and there but for the grace of God goes every man jack of us. What I wish to make plain, is that he constantly drifted from the golden mean. I am not sure if he was born with it, and grew into it, but his temperament inclined to the Juvenalian rather than the Horatian, particularly in terms of his response to the fair sex. He loved to contemplate, and consequently to generate, outrage, and he would surround himself with colour and intensity. There was a manipulative ferocity about him, of which I myself was a victim and on occasion simultaneously a witness. He would make old people and children perform their adulation of him, he would goad young women to express their disgust at his flagrant and coarse advances, he would make old men weep and young men fall silent. He called this his 'field work', yet when he attempted to record these exchanges, in other words when he came to reiterate in language what he had perpetrated in fact, much was lost in the re-telling, or more plainly when he told me what he had seen and done his words would envelop everything including himself, in a terrible mist of verbiage. He could not call a spade a bloody shovel. It was not a simple attitude of arrogance on his part which made him do this, it resembled rather a nervous indisposition, something approaching an intellectual form of autism, as it were.

Perhaps it was his belief, a belief he always reiterated when drunk, that he was incapable of thinking himself into another person's shoes, or should I say head, yes, perhaps that's what gave him his intense thirst for finding out about people. In that sense he married himself to a hopeless project from the start, his profession was also his nemesis. But I must not get ahead of myself, and beyond this it is dismal, indeed abjectly depressing, to talk of this subject, owing to the fact that, despite his undoubted energy, he went about everything so ponderously. He could not be designated an old fashioned bore, exactly, but he used to drive me to distraction owing to his total inability ever to get to the point. In this his mind was like his body. He was physically cumbersome, and his motions mirrored his speech. Every movement was the product of a slow and complete certainty born out of massive deliberation. One suspected that he had forced himself to move in precisely an equivalent manner to that in which he had forced himself to think; and that the harmony had been achieved at a terrible price. It was, perhaps, precisely the sense of troubled unions which made him so fascinating. He emanated the impression most strongly that what one saw was most definitely not what one got, a phenomenon always intriguing, not to say beautiful to behold. Behavioural predictability in an individual always exasperates me, I am a great believer in the duende, and I perpetually had the sense that one day he would burst out, the incarnation of the spirit of the duende itself. My reasons for such optimism lay in the possibility that the painfully distilled rationality which lay behind his everyday life might have been just a curtain, a curtain which kept in obscurity a terrific, a chaotic, underlife of thought, a dark flash tide which threatened to pounce upon and engulf all his carefully laid plans. One certainly had the impression that this might be the case on more than one occasion. One felt that it was not inconceivable that there might be a part of him which was involved in a desolate perversity, he looked at the most perfect innocence as a reformed alcoholic would look at a bottle of vintage champagne. The horror lay in the fact that it was precisely that part of him which also made him terrified of carrying regularity too far, of becoming the slave of routine. He was, quite rightly, terrified of the internecine process by which people become completely an extension of their habits. His mind was torn, and the result was that his ponderous determination was married to a certain, one might say a necessary, spasmodic quality. He might suddenly change direction, it might be over a woman, or over a cause, but the effect was always the same, and it was at these rare points, and only at these points, that one really felt that one saw the whole of him. He appeared in his totality at the moment when he had thrown in the towel.

Let me give an example, a very recent example. Among his prolonged fads he had ended up spending a good deal of time in South Africa, just before the end of Apartheid. When that system, unbelievably and some might argue not entirely beneficially, fell apart, his interest began to break up as well. Maybe he was a victim of circumstance, but I saw a deeper current at work. You see he had been living on and off for several years, although by then a virtual cripple, in a tin shack with a family of six poor, uneducated and he would, I presume, add, beautiful and completely exhilarating, black people. It constituted some sort of a search for a home and family, he had long ago ceased lusting after the young tribeswomen, for reasons which will become apparent. His devotion to the two older daughters now had about it a sort of Dickensian sentimentality and philanthropic amplitude. He paid for the oldest children's college education and in return he lay on a camp bed, almost totally immobile, and watched the comings and goings, dressings and undressings, who could ask for more? But behind it all there was also the idea that these people could be helped, and he would do all that he could to drag them out of the mire. With the dismantling of the hated system of oppression it came to the crunch, after freedom came, the squatter townships became even more violent and even more closed down. He had always believed in the struggle, but he had always been quite candid in his assessment that an economic sectarianism of unparalleled barbarity would be the consequence of the end of Apartheid.

Those with nothing were now utterly sealed off from the new socially mobile black middle classes, and there appeared he informed me, through the stern lenses of political common sense, little room even for hoping that one could get out. Perhaps, with an even exaggerated severity, he inferred that there was no longer anyone to blame, Nelson Mandela being, to all intents and purposes, beyond the normal contexts of analysis, and beyond accountability. Indeed the Western Shibboleth erected around Mandela, and not necessarily even a simulacrum of his proper self, might be seen most accurately as the late twentieth century resurrection of the spirit of William Wilberforce, the slave's champion, an individual sanctified by public opinion, the subject of universal hagiography. Well it was at that juncture in South Africa's violent history that my Australian's interest evaporated, it was at this point that he walked away. Well hardly walked, he was carried in a sort of home built sedan chair to the taxi, and then flew off. And the way he explained his action was quite horrible. He looked at me, and slowly shaking his head, an action which required that he slowly shake his entire body from side to side, he stated: 'I suddenly saw that they were all a bunch of complete losers, quite simply the losers'. He endowed that final word with a weight of monumental failure, a weight from under which no one was ever going to be allowed to crawl out alive. There was no pity in his voice, and not even a trace of humour, merely a dry and disinterested certainty. Then the conversation moved on, we were having lunch at the time.

Whether this tendency to walk away was cowardice, good sense, or even petulance, was not easy to assess. One would imagine that as far as he was aware of what was going on, something we never know, he saw it as a good deal more than bad luck. His prolonged obsessive attractions to certain causes and certain places, meant that his life would be held down in one place or another while the spell lasted. When I say the spell this, associatively, brings me to the heart of the matter, the part that fascinated me the most. He believed in magic, and I mean real grown up magic, and he did not believe magic to be confined to other people in remote lands, not just some notion of respect for a whole load of mumbo jumbo, darkies prancing round the spurting blood of a decapitated goat or cockerel, that sort of thing. No, he had gone into the whole matter very deeply indeed, perhaps far too deeply. He had, somewhat unwittingly, met his comeuppance in the most unexpected quarter. Whether it was magic he experienced, or simply an ability to empathise with a culture so strangely different from ours, I am not sure. Yet here is the story at last.

Some thirty years before the South African episode he called unexpectedly at my rooms one summer afternoon. My arm was in plaster up to the elbow, following a genuinely quite worrying laceration to my thumb, the result of an overzealous attempt to quarter a pheasant with an insufficiently sharpened game carving knife. The wound had required neurological surgery to restore sensation to the damaged digit. I was sitting reading, again, my favourite section of *Lesbia Brandon* when what looked like a tramp passed my window in the sunlight. He was a big corpulent man, despite the fact that the head was bowed, he stooped almost double, and as his coat flapped in the wind I glimpsed an enormous pair of trousers, that gave the peculiar effect of having been sculpted in stone. A knock at the door followed, perfectly audible owing to the fact that, despite the day, I was sporting my oak.

Before me stood my Australian, he looked most unwell, to be honest he looked shattered, an unacceptable mess, and somehow no longer of this World. He moved with even greater deliberation than I remembered, and had the utmost difficulty in levering himself into a chair. The peculiar trousers which I had glimpsed were much in evidence. They were bluish grey and immensely stiff. They looked as if they were made out of asbestos. When I mentioned this to him he replied that this was in fact the case, they were very old fashioned fireman's trousers constructed in the 1930s. He claimed they kept his tackle dry in the jungles of South America.

As he sat I examined the joints of his fingers closely, they were not swollen but he was almost unable to clasp them around the cup of coffee I gave him. He also had a revolting pallor to his face, smooth and desiccated. He looked stale but he smelled anything but, he smelled positively delicious, as if he had drenched himself in some form of exotic aftershave. He had been working in an obscure part of Latin America for several years, and I imagined he had been bitten by some obscure form of hellish bug, a venchuga fly, or that infamous horned beetle called by some Indian tribes the mother of all the snakes. It wasn't clear to me what he had been up to, except that it was all about magic again. We had one of our long conversations which eventually, as so often, returned to the subject of enchantment, and I asked him if he was still bewitched. He replied, in a tone of ineffable stiffness, that he didn't know, that perhaps there was now no way of finding out, but that he would never see things in quite the same way again. He then settled into his story. He described how, travelling alone, he had wandered in the Amazon jungle and had come across the most remarkable community of people, all of them blind from birth, a blind tribe who called themselves the Hoimet, blind for generations, it seemed possible that they had always been blind. They inhabited a pocket of land somewhere in the murky area between the borders of Brazil and Paraguay. The Hoimet lived within an enormous and beautifully cultivated set of gardens, in land which had been cleared before they settled in this area. They moved with remarkable slowness, much in the manner of the three toed sloth, which also inhabits this part of the jungle. They smeared their bodies with ashes, believing fire to be a sacred substance and believing that it's spirit lurked within the ashes. These were not normal ashes, but ashes that glistened like silver, they called these ashes the shining smoke. The Hoimet had taught my Australian many things. For example one day he had asked them how they saw him, given that they only knew him through what they felt and what they heard. This is when the story proper was told, I only recorded him from this point, after the incidental details which I have just alluded to had been given out. I recorded his conversation, as I often did. He was a fluent, an appallingly fluent, speaker, especially when drunk. I give the transcript of the tape virtually unchanged:

'When I asked them why they talked of colours so much they replied: "The voices all have a colour. The voices of the living have dark colours, thin colours and weak colours, and the voices of the dead have the thick and strong colours, the warm, the hot, the burning colours". So not only sound had colour for these people, but touch had colour as well, and as I was to find, the dead had colour in particular. You look puzzled, let me explain. Death is not like death in our world. The whole Hoimet society lives in the presence of the dead, in fact you might say that death is at the heart of their life, it is the heart of the matter, and everything grows through it. Their manner of life and their manner of death are outside the rules we live by. They would be deemed self destructive and criminally solipsistic lunatics in a Western court of law, but I became increasingly seduced by the simple justice and transparent beauties of their customs.

The Hoimet burial grounds are bang in the middle of everything, and they are laid out in the following manner. But before I go on let me explain, at this point, that the topography cannot be set out without reference to the ideas behind it, the thought and custom which justify it. You see no one here dies of natural causes. When an individual is tired of life, and I mean this quite literally, people here at any age just get tired of the whole business, then they go through the following procedure. First off they compose a song, or sort of poem, in which they enumerate the seventeen things which gave them the most pleasure in their former life. This song is a paradoxically ghastly creation, because the things which delighted them now fill them with horror, they now cause them a pain which is difficult to explain and impossible to comprehend. You see when the terrible greyness falls upon them, which they call the state of 'Heeve', they are not simply indifferent to their former pleasures, but they are keenly aware of the distance they have fallen.

Or to put it another way they look upon the former joy of life as one who is trapped, drowning, beneath the frozen ice stares out at the sunlight which still gloriously, shines through, is diffracted through, the fatal rigid and frigid curtain which will bring death. It is not a spiritual inebriety I am talking of, an insensate dementia, but something infinitely worse, something beyond what we, here and now, in our world of reason and unreason, are permitted to understand. What they die by and what they live through in the process cannot be bundled under any of our convenient labels, the blanket term of depression has no place in their world. The state of extreme but painfully hyper-active boredom into which they all, at one point or another fall, is an horrifically wired up tedium, a living death shot through with wild lights. It is as if the mind of the young Dorothy Wordsworth, keen, living, breathing, capable of putting into a few words the cleanly inspired perceptions of genius, were forced into obscene cohabitation with the dull madwoman that she became. As if the two women were fused in the present, no distance, no separation, yet the madness decides that death is the only preferred option. Or maybe even that is a presumptuous attempt at equivalence on my part. I cannot put into words what happens when the 'Heeve' descends, or arrives, or takes over, or comes into being, lives and breathes its short life within a person. All that is certain is the non negotiability. Heeve is not something to be treated, like our myths of depression. It is something given, a horribly alive negativity, that arrives in the same sense that life arrives, a sort of obscene libation which death grudgingly, perhaps simperingly, gives way to, before the horrible abstraction of its finality. These people live then a different existence, an existence where everyone is doomed, or privileged, to find and to endure the experience of a space between life and death, a sort of throbbing cord, where they realise that in order to die they must learn to abhor the intensities of life.

I can't go on trying to set it out, I could give some examples, tell you some stories, but I don't want to, like I say, there are no words, I will stick to facts. So the man, woman, girl or boy who gets the 'Heeve' sits down, in the state of an intensely engaged imaginative and spiritual desolation beyond our wildest dreams, to compose a song of sorrow, seventeen intricate verses giving seventeen delights. Seventeen is a sacred number, and the peon to 'Heeve' is then performed by seventeen people, with seventeen sets of seventeen stringed instruments, in a cycle of seventeen notes. And then the one who has decided to die, or who is outside life and death, demands to be given 'Yalip.' Yalip is intimately related to 'Heeve' and is as damnably difficult to itemise. Yalip is both a concept to the Hoimet, and is physically embodied in a substance. Materially it is a type of tree gum, a resin, which is not only highly toxic but which has peculiar preservative qualities. It runs like, and is the colour of, quicksilver, and the stuff is also a powerful psychotropic drug, and taken in small amounts blows the doors and windows of perception right out of the building. But to get back to the point, the 'Heevorfil', or person who is to go, drinks a large amount of this stuff, measured in a strange tree bark container like a tulip bulb, at least a couple of pints I'd reckon. They then die in ecstasy or in the most appalling agony, it is impossible to predict which, you just have to trust to luck it seems. Hence Yalip is represented in a mask which carries an orgasmic expression, it is impossible to tell if it expresses pain or pleasure. That's the point.

The body then slowly begins to embalm itself, as the Yalip soaks gradually through all the tissues. Eventually even the bones absorb it. Yalip is an immensely complicated protein, which, like egg yolk, eternally hardens. During the first two years the effects are barely perceptible on the corpse. The flesh is, however, incapable of decay, even the eyes, miraculously, retain their lustre. After about twenty years the body, while flexible is as hard as wood to the touch. After fifty years the body may still be manipulated, but possesses an adamantine toughness. After one hundred years it begins to develop the most remarkable sheen, and the whole ensemble begins to turn into a gleaming silver grey, very much like iron pyrites.

Well long before this, after seventeen times seven sunrises, the body, or mummy, or whatever the earthly remains now are, is taken up. A crystal hook is put through the left ear, and the whole object is suspended from one of the trees of life, immense hardwood trees, up to three hundred feet high, which are hung with hundreds of these monumental corpses. The trees are all planted, or were all planted, in pear shapes, about sixty yards apart, in the centre of the ritual gardens of death, or life. All vegetation around them is burned every seventeen full moons, in order to enrich the soil and to clean the landscape, the gigantic trees are too vast to be affected by such minimal vegetable combustion.

As soon as the fires die down they celebrate a day of the dead. They rub their hands and feet, which are already of a peculiar sensitivity, upon a specially prepared block of volcanic rock, which thins the skin excessively, it must be almost to the point where the division between inside and outside in perceptual terms, ceases to exist. They have a phrase which defines the point at which the skin is thin enough, and before blood is drawn, and this point is called 'feeling the air', I think that they mean this quite literally, that at a certain point the body literally feels the air. I noticed when I watched one of their infants a few moments after it was born, that its first instinctive action, though the tiny thing was completely blind, was to reach out and feel the air, rub it gently though miniature fingers, as if it was so much dough. I believe they are capable of regaining such sensitivity through recourse to the pumice rock, although their skin inevitably hardens slightly as they grow. I am reluctant to speculate on this point, because they found my epidermis noxious, coarse, malodorous and downright laughable. To them I appeared covered in cow hide, and for their purpose I could feel nothing, and I smelt both nothing and disgusting, in terms of their perception. But I did my best to understand it all. Anyway, having reached this state, they then anoint themselves with Yalip upon the centre of the palm of their left hand, and one small area of the tip of the penis, or the labia, and this applies to individuals of all ages. They then cover themselves with the shining ashes, and lie still in a great heap, staring, if that is what blind people do, at the sky, until the moon ceases to be visible, or until the sun rises, whichever happens first. I have to confess that I only witnessed the ceremony, under special dispensation, upon one occasion, when I agreed myself to participate in all particulars. I can't really remember that much, a screaming headache, and a whirling grey form, like a grey Catherine wheel in my sight, or behind my eyes. Then no more.

The next morning, feeling none the worse for wear, I walked down to the river bank, which bordered upon the most beautiful of their gardens. The gentle slope was set about with gleaming smooth rails, and the rails let into gaps, lovely little pools where the water sat, and where the women did their washing. I walked down and saw two young pregnant women, both the same age and about six or seven months pregnant, washing clothes in the river together, standing stark naked with all this washing on the stones, pounding and pounding away. They were engaged in a fierce dispute and were pointing in an animated way at each others breasts. One had substantial pear shaped breasts, and the other had these little pointy ones like ice cream cones. It was strange, to my anthropologists eye, to see such variety of form within a single tribe, which made me speculate that perhaps these people were the result of the amalgamation of more than one Indian people. I also suddenly thought that this was the first occasion on which I had ever seen any of the adults unclothed, their exceptional modesty was a continual part of their behaviour. When they sensed me and turned to me they immediately covered themselves with the wet washing. When I asked them what the trouble was they explained. The one with big breasts had been complaining to the one with the small breasts, that it really hurt her to pound, because of the bouncing movement it caused, and that it was really terrible, it went on and on, and nothing could be done. The other said that it was as bad for her, her breasts might be smaller and firmer, but they moved quicker, and harder as a result. They then looked slyly, and I thought imploringly with their blind eyes, at me, and suggested that I should adjudicate between them, and that holding their breasts while they worked was my only option. I have to say the prospect was not altogether disheartening, they were two fine looking young women, although I have to say in all honesty I have always preferred ice cream cones to pears, although stewed pears and ice cream is a peculiar favourite of mine.

I walked down the grass and slowly put my hands beneath the gently swaying breasts of the pear shaped one. And I thought, as I made this dual movement with my hands, that I had never touched one of the bodies of these people before, that in fact every gesture and every movement of theirs had prescribed any possibility of such intimacy. I had, in fact, never seen any one of them touch any other, they did not kiss, they had no customary observance requiring contact, such as, for example, hand shaking. And then, in the full enormity of this realisation I placed, simultaneously, my hand on each breast, and found them to be as moist and pliant as fresh raw fillet steak and as hard as wood. I then lost consciousness. I came back to the world to find myself with a large bruise on my left temple lying alone in the jungle, not far from a Brazilian charcoal burning settlement. Five days later I was able to take a small plane out to São Paulo.'

We both knew that the story was over. He stared out disconsolately towards me, his grey shining eyes expressed what I can only describe as intense boredom.

BLACK

We walk in through the door with two uniformed police, a young man and a young woman. There is a sickening fug, a smell so intensely bad that the two Rozzers are holding their noses most theatrically. They look strangely like the workman who sits in the scaffolding above the stage in the famous rising shot at the opera in *Citizen Kane*. In the corner of the room to the right of the Rozzers is a black pile, a real mess. A ghetto blaster is turned on in the left hand corner of the room and is playing, on low volume, Mick Jagger singing 'I see a red door and I want it painted black, no colour any more I want it painted black.' Like the Police, going in, at first we can't believe our eyes, at first it doesn't look like a body, let alone two. It looks just like nothing on Earth, a big black heap of rags and shit in the corner. My God, it's got a smell to it though. The music goes on and the police woman intones above, or around, it:

'To think that people worth that much money could do that to themselves, it just doesn't make sense. It makes you feel sick, dizzy in the brain. It smells like nothing on earth.'

The other Rozzer takes up the cue:

'Is nobody safe any more? How did it happen that such a happy couple could have been embalmed in black toilet paper, in black *used* toilet paper, and who ever heard of black toilet paper anyway?'

It's a long dark story, let us begin.

It's hard to tell how it started, maybe it was that bad conversation. The last time Busy talked to Pete, things had gone wrong, really quite badly wrong. Busy was drunk, but thought that he knew Pete well enough for him not to mind when Busy forgot the name of his wife and daughter. But Pete was the kind of person who demands that you have a go at their names, and then listens for the answer, so Busy had a go, and got it wrong, way wrong. Busy was sure that they were called George and Dombie, George being short for Georgina and Dombie short for Dominic. When you go for, or try to sniff out, something as precious as the abbreviations, then you are really chancing your arm. I suppose that Busy should have accepted the consequences of, quite literally, taking these people for something else, taking their names in vain, all because of a couple of bottles of quite a cheap white Rioja. Busy was way off line, missed the target by a mile, went off too early, like a vicar in a brothel, and was hoist with his own petard. There came upon the phone line this complete silence. A barbed wire silence, a real over the top, first day of the Somme, machine gun nest and mustard gas, body parts in the mud and air, human bits flying everywhere, flares at midnight, Paschendale, Verdun, Assassination of the Archduke, von Schlieffan plan, friend and foe playing football on Christmas day with an old cabbage, All Quiet on the Western Front, barbed wire, silence..

###
###
######## well ################## that ###################### barbedwiresilence
###
lasted for ### nearly
six years. And it destroyed Busy and Dolene. Rat-tat-tat-tat-tat-tat-tat. It was a creeping
death, a freezing mist, a white silence, a white noise, and there was no way out of it, and
no way through it, the end of a friendship and the end of a life, Do and Biz, well hell, they
just turned in on themselves, and could only do the housework.
    'You do upstairs, and I'll do downstairs.'
    Said Busy.
    'No, we'll do it together, it's more relaxing that way.'
    Replied Dolene, and continued.
    'Put on a tape, that one of Phil Spectre's greatest hits, you know the wall of sound, it
helps drown out the vacuum cleaner.'
    'Look at the state of this carpet, Do.'
    Busy said.
    'It's really running to seed, it's, well it's completely impregnated with shit.'
    'That's a nasty thought.'
    Said Dolene.
    'Well it's the honest to God truth, it's like Juno came down in the guise of a turd and
had sex with his carpet, just spraying his seed around this way and that.'
    'That's a dirty thought.'
    Said Dolene.
    'Well don't just stand there gawking, get swabbing.'
    Said Biz, and went on.
    'It wasn't always this way Do.'
    'Biz I remember the days when you could have mistaken this place for a wedding cake.'
    'Oh, don't go on so Do.'
    'But Biz, when did we start to live like slobs?'
    'Do, I'm afraid that it isn't that simple, we really are slobs we ain't just acting at it, the
place is a midden, a cess pool, a genuine and real cloaca Tophet pit, a dark dive into the
slimy side of effluence.'
    'But sometimes Biz I look back over the years and I think it's not all our own fault.'
    'The house had a spirit of its own. My God it's an evil place, it took us over, it played
fast and loose, we never stood a chance, we never had a ghost of a chance.'
    And maybe Biz and Do do have a point. It was a small house, and they had bought it
cheap, in a state of terrible disrepair, not long after the terrible freak accident with gas and
some kind of a faulty cooker had done for the former owners. It had been in the local
paper, a strange case, two poor dead human bodies, two people blown to kingdom come.
Terrible remains on the carpet, burned up things that looked like the victims of some terrorist attack or something. As Busy had observed, with passion and a rare sense of occasion, when the estate agent had shown them the photo:
    'You just would not think that a buggered up domestic appliance could do that to a
normal human being, you'd think that it would have had to be something spectacular, and
that Jerry Adams, or Mohammed Al Fayed Dali, or some other terrorist celebrity would
have been on telly talking it through with everyone, not just a leaky main and a match,
and then a photo in the local rag.'
    But strange to relate Busy and Dolene had got off to a bright start. Perhaps because the
place had this aura of being smoked out and burned black and blue Biz and Do had decided
to start off and put everything bang to whites.
    'Let's make this the most Bristol fashion and ship shape, cheerful Englishman's castle
in the whole of the Essex delta.'
    Said Biz gaily.

They bought a polar white washing machine, and a polar white fridge, that stood there, a pristine and handsome rectangle, perfectly polar, like a block of ice flown straight in from a glacier. As precious a lump as that very block of Carrara marble, just waiting for Michelangelo's David to spring out of it. They bought sixty litres of trade-standard-polar-white-gloss-emulsion, and set to laying down coat after coat of paint, on the walls, ceiling and floor. The more coats they put on, the more polar white it became. On a sunny summer's day they had to wear their designer shades to keep out the glare, it even felt a shade or two colder than an ordinary house. Whenever Busy went out to get a paper he always said:

'I'm just going out for a whaz and I may be some time.'

Just like the famous Captain Titus Oates, as Do always said. How they chuckled.

One day Dolene could not hack it any longer. She began throwing things around, the whiteness was bearing down on her brain with a terrible pressure, white noise, white water, the polar water torture. It all began with an argument over whose turn it was to put the jar of red pesto in the Polar white fridge. With an icy stare and the groan of a wolf howling upon the Bothnic main, Do launched the pesto, a comestible hand grenade, and it exploded against the wall. The next thing was an over blown food fight, and the house was never polar white again. Meal times became obsessive, every remaining spot of white in the kitchen had to be obliterated with left-overs. It was as if an evil Genie had escaped from a bottle, the spirit of a former age, forcing them to foul their own nest, to shit on their own sheets. After one meal they lay back looking at God's handy work leaking down the walls:

'My God Do, what a shit heap.'

'We really have crapped on our own front doorstep this time, Biz.'

'Yep, we really have pee'd in our own back yard.'

'Well, at least there's absolutely nothing to be seen of that polar white shit any more, although, yes indeedee, I do spot a nasty little white spot. Up and at'em, that dot up to the left of the lamp shade, hit it with the marmite bagel Dolene.'

Do aims her bagel, taking the martial stance of a Greek javelin thrower, and lets fly. The bagel is coated in marmite from head to foot, as if it were some sacrifice at the centre of a sinister ritual. She flings it at the ceiling, it obliterates the offending spot and falls thickly into a corner, hitting an enormous packet of lavatory paper.

A terrible silence falls and they look at each other, then slowly over at the packet of paper rolls, marked, POLAR WHITE in pitch black lettering, at least four inches high.

'O sweet Jesus that's disgusting.'

Says Dolene.

'Wipe it out, wipe it off the face of the Earth, now and forever more, amen.'

Roars Busy, with the ferocity of an Olango missionary. He then checks himself, and adds more reflectively:

'Do this time we've got our work cut out. This is a new territory, virgin terrain, a new world to conquer.'

'Oh, Brave New World, Biz.'

'Not, so fast Do. This is a big problem, muito, muito big. I mean it's a meaty one, a problem with our entire culture, a missing link, and now I think about it, it stinks to high heaven, it stinks of mortality. Think about it, it's little short of a racist slur upon our neck of the woods. I ask you in all seriousness, Do, when did you last wipe your arse with a piece of black paper?'

Do's eyes widen, they look big, innocent and frightened, just like a doe, she says, thrilling to every syllable:

'Biz you've called their bluff this time, you're really onto something big.'

Biz isn't going to be sucked into the hysteria of the moment, he was made for this hour, he checks his brain out and takes one giant mental step backwards:

'Alright Do, cool it, cool it, these are the days that try men's souls, the eleven o'clock revolutionary can get on his bike. I must stand back, get the bigger picture, tack in the general composition with the big bushy brush. Let me summarise, give you the lay of the land, suggest a battle plan. There you are, shopping list in hand, and it reads, LOO PAPER. It looks innocent enough, my God it was innocent enough until today. But now we know, for all the appearance of freedom, and liberality, that there is a dark social contract lodged within the underbelly of intolerance, nursing a viper in its very vitals. You cannot walk in off the street, into a supermarket, or even a little grocer's, or a local news agent, and buy yourself a roll of black loo paper. It's just not possible for the hideous reason, that they quite simply don't make it. Our job is to stand up and push it a leetle bit further, and to demand, in all decency, why it is not made? No rhyme or reason, Do, no excuses offered, no rhyme or reason at all.'

'It's a puzzler alright, and no bloody point to it.'

'Indeed Do. But beyond this is the argument that it's paper apartheid, and we will have no names apart. As I say, you can go in and ask them for lemon or lime or teapot blue, or rose pink, I've seen lilac they even put scent on it, and I've smelt the abominable stuff, and I've seen peach, ivory and reams of the polar white stuff. But no black, ono, shit and black, for some strange reason, have landed way outside the pale, out of order, a bridge too far, a straw upon the camel's back. It is paper apartheid.'

'Biz, this could be too big for the two of us to handle, do we need outside help?'

'Do, don't rush me. Let me come at it another way, by indirection shall we flush directions down and out. Do ray me so far café latte Do… what colour are your knickers today?'

Do nods sagaciously, she smells which way the wind's blowing:

'I'm wearing the black thong today Biz, and I ask you straight to your face, what colour are yours?'

'I'm wearing one of my three hundred and sixty pairs of black boxers Do, the ones with Tyson's face on them, as per usual.'

'There you are, black knickers, no problem, some people would even say they were sexy, you can wipe your arse with a pair of black knickers and no one gives a shit, but where can you get a roll of black arse wipes?'

'No way Do, and it's a bloody disgrace, it would be a gift to humanity at large if someone out there started to put things to rights, some big cheese, or a person with a vision, a captain of industry, a seer, a voyeur.'

'Biz it's time to name and shame, society has been beating about the bush for way too long.'

'Nail on the head, name and shame Do.'

After a few more seconds of awed silence Biz continues:

'Today is a big day Do, one of the biggest, today we have cracked it, and heads will roll. Biz, our life's work lies steadily before us, and we start with that starched white polar shit paper, let's tie die it black, let's ensable it, and then let's wipe it to death, wipe it till its bloody nose bleeds.'

Easier said than done of course. It takes months of painful experiment, a forensic dabbling in mediums and pigments. Do and Biz are hunting, each intent to track down the black that sticks, the black that can saturate, that will obliterate, that would do in their pet hate and mortal foe on contact, for ever and ever. For Biz it's the super soft super white non recycled de luxe brands that she hates with a passion. These fat succulent papers fill Biz with disgust, they smack of privilege, waste, soft eating on soft beds, they smack of a kind of slackness and luxury that could only come out of the richer things of life. 'Quilted' she mutters, the voice of capitalism is writ over large in that one word. Strange to say for Do it is the other way round, the hatred goes straight at the thin, shiny little rectangle that reeks of disinfectant and institutionalised defecation. The full catastrophe of Jays tissue, not even white, but translucent, like flayed skin from some terrible experiment in the dungeons of a far away dictatorship. Yet only weeks after the initial excitement had worn off, through sheer will power, and stern application, they had arrived at a workable, maybe even the final, solution.

All good things come to an end, sheer hubris of course. And now we join them in real time, as they sit, with eyes as pink and angry as the newly scrubbed gills of a cleaned mackerel. They have dragged themselves to the local pub, and drink their pints of thick black stout. We become aware of the intolerable sounds of a suffering babe. It shrieks, it wails with the out of body intensity of real pain.

'A bad case of nappy rash, no doubt.'

Says Do.

In slow motion we see a distracted mother move over to a large Polar white bag. She picks out of it, with long slender polar white fingers, a polar white plastic box. She opens the lid and takes out a polar white nappy and sets to work changing the baby's bottom, rubbing polar white cream into the infant crack. Do and Biz exchange an anguished look, their bottom lips tremble, they shake their heads, and, of one mind and in a single movement, they rise. Hand in hand the wend their weary way home.

Scene, the front room, time two thirty A.M., empty bottles of white Rioja lying around like corpses on a battlefield.

Thousands of miles of died black, dried black, toilet tissue festooned, an orgy of coiled mating snakes. Iridescent along its terrible serpentine lengths, unspeakable moist stains. Biz, walking like a film zombie, trips over the ghetto blaster, set on a loop, which begins to play their favourite song, the Stones 'Painted Black'. Solemnly Do and Biz begin to wind the sepulchral spirals of stinking paper about each others limp forms, winding slowly, ritualistically, anti-clockwise. They have lost the will to carry the torch, to take the fight to the enemy. The last we see of them are two flailing mummies in the corner, the two lines of the tune we heard at the beginning repeat themselves endlessly. The last we hear of Do and Biz is a muffled chant, it sounds like 'Me at last, me at last, Good Lord Almighty, me at last'. Well, well, well.